the cupcake witch

THE CHANCELLOR FAIRY TALES, BOOK 2

MELANIE KARSAK

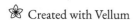 Created with Vellum

"Follow your bliss & don't be afraid & doors will open where you didn't know they were going to be."
Joseph Campbell

julie

Holding the whisk tightly, I swirled the pale-yellow batter around the bowl, the sweet scents of vanilla, brown sugar, and bitter dark chocolate perfuming the air. Even though it was a cool autumn morning, the heat from the oven made the kitchen feel toasty warm. I'd been baking all morning: expresso mini cupcakes with cappuccino flavored frosting, matcha green tea macaroons, and strawberry rhubarb coffee cake. The kitchen smelled divine. Now, with a pot of coffee brewing and a batch of chocolate chip walnut cookies just about ready to go into the oven, I could almost relax.

"Here, taste this," I said to Dad, scooping up a small bite of the dough with a spoon and sticking it into his mouth before he could protest.

"You're going to give me salmonella poisoning," he said then sighed deeply. "A little food poisoning is worth it. So good, but they taste...different."

"Bad different?"

Dad shook his head. "Tasty different."

"Organic brown sugar and sea salt."

"I'm going to gain ten pounds before you go back to college next week," he said with a laugh then turned back to his paperwork.

Sighing, I placed the cookie dough on the baking sheet and stuck it in the oven. How was I going to tell Dad I wasn't planning on going back? With Mom gone... well, I just didn't even know why I was there anymore. It wasn't like I had ever wanted to go to college. I wanted to be a baker. But Mom wanted me to be a dentist, so I was studying pre-dentistry. Now, Mom was gone. The pain of her loss still felt like a huge lump in my chest.

I poured Dad and myself a coffee and sat down at the table. He was thumbing through a heap of real estate briefs. Dayton Real Estate was busier than ever, and with Mom gone, an agent short. Dad was running himself ragged.

I spooned some raw sugar into my cup and tried to think of something to say other than the fact that I hated school. It was nearly the end of October and thus far junior year had been a bust. I told Dad I wasn't ready.

After losing Mom that summer, I just couldn't get my head back into the game. I didn't want to waste my life pursuing a career in dentistry just because everyone, but especially Mom, thought it would be a good move for a smart girl like me. Mom's death had taught me many things, the most important being that life was short. Why was I working so hard for a future I felt pretty apathetic about?

"Here is the property in Chancellor I was telling you about," Dad said, saving me from having the dreaded conversation once more, as he handed me an envelope. From inside, I pulled out a yellowed photograph of a tiny little Tudor-style cottage. Under the photo, the words *Serendipity Gardens* had been written in faded pencil.

"It looks like a witch's cottage. Mrs. Aster, the woman who left us the building...how did you say we were related again?" I stared at the photograph as I twirled one red dreadlock around my finger. The little building was a mess, the glass nursery overgrown, but there was something quaint, almost fairy tale like, about it.

Dad was eyeing the table full of sweets, finally settling on one of the mini cupcakes, popping it into his mouth. "These are amazing, Julie. Seriously," he said after a moment. "Mrs. Aster was Grandma Belle's husband's sister."

"And how does that make her related to us?"

"Through marriage only, but we are her closest living relatives," Dad said then shrugged. "I've got the property into the MLS system, but I need to run over to Chancellor this week and put up the signs. Probably won't be hard to move the old place. I already have a message—which I haven't even managed to return yet—from Blushing Grape Vineyards inquiring on the property. Need to get that sign up, see if I can fish any other bids out of the pond. Maybe the college will want the property, turn it into an office or something. On the corner of Main Street and Magnolia, the location is great. We'll probably get a good price if we can get some competition," Dad said then paused. He looked up at me, a serious expression on his face. "You know, Chancellor College offers science degrees. Jules, I know you aren't happy..." he began then stopped. Trying again, he switched directions by saying, "Maybe if you were closer to home, things might be easier."

Panicking, I picked up the envelope. "Chancellor, eh? Don't they have a harvest festival at this time of year? Why don't I take the signs over? I'll grab a pumpkin spice latte or something."

My dad pushed his glasses back up his nose then ran his hand through his hair. Was it my imagination or did his hair look whiter? His face was undoubtedly more drawn. He must have shed twenty pounds from his already thin frame. Mom's death had hit us both hard. It was just manifesting differently. Dad was running thin, and I was running scared. I didn't want to waste my life following the dream Mom had laid out so neatly for me. My real passion had always lain in the kitchen. Fondant. Buttercream. Meringue. Ever since I got my first Easy-Bake Oven, I knew what I wanted to do, who I wanted to be. My dream, however, had never jelled with what Mom had wanted. And as much as it hurt, Mom was gone. I could keep going to college for her, but that didn't feel right. I needed to do something. Something needed to change. And in the meantime, I was failing my classes.

"Walk around the campus while you're there. Check out its vibe. See if you like it."

"Or not," I said absently. The last thing I wanted was more college: more homework I couldn't get myself to complete, more classes I couldn't get myself to go to, more anything.

"You know, they also have a culinary program," my dad said carefully. "A letter came from your college's advising office. It said you're failing all—"

"I...I know," I stammered, standing. "Can we talk about it tonight?"

He nodded. "I love you. We're both just trying to

manage here." He lifted a macaroon then looked from it to me. "The culinary program. Mom and I always disagreed...tonight, let's talk. But you're making dinner."

"Of course. It's pizza night! I bought portabella mushrooms, arugula, and goat cheese."

"You had me at portabella," Dad said with a chuckle. "Anything would be better than those damned frozen dinners."

"Dad! You can't eat that garbage."

He shrugged. "What can I say? I don't have time to cook. Speaking of which, did you know it only takes five weeks to get a real estate license? Without your mom, I could use the extra help," he said then patted the massive stack of inspection reports, loan documents, and other paperwork that was my dad's—and had been my mom's—life's work, "and a home cooked meal, on occasion."

I picked up the envelope then kissed my dad on his balding head. "Home-cooked meals I can handle."

My dad patted my hand.

"Take the cookies out when the timer goes off?"

"Of course. I'd never let a Julie Dayton cookie burn. Too precious a commodity."

I wrapped my arms around my dad and hugged him tightly.

"Love you," I said.

"Love you too, Julie bean," he replied.

Letting him go, I grabbed my purse and keys and headed off to the witch's cottage.

CHAPTER 2

horatio

"**F**abulous event, Horatio," Mrs. White, the wife of the President of Chancellor College said, shaking my hand as she left the pristine white tent situated on the small public beach at Chancellor Park.

"Thank you so much. It was a pleasure to see you and President White again."

She smiled nicely then headed to the parking lot where a limo waited to take her and her husband, who was also shaking hands as he made his way to the limo, back to the college.

I inhaled deeply and looked out at the lake. The morning sunlight was shimmering on the dark blue waves. There was a chill in the air, but it wasn't too windy yet. I had pulled it off. When my sister, Viola, had volunteered me to organize the annual charity breakfast and fundraiser for the Chancellor Arts Council, I wanted to kill her. But the champagne breakfast had gone off without a hitch, and we'd raised more than two hundred and fifty thousand dollars that morning for youth arts programs.

"I don't want to say I told you so, but I told you so," a soft voice said, followed by a playful punch in the arm.

I opened my eyes and grinned at Viola who looked, admittedly, very pretty in her Merlot-colored "Hillary Clinton"—as she had called it—suit. Her dark hair glimmered in the sunlight, reflecting tints of blue.

"I just got a bunch of old broads liquored up on mimosas and begged for money for kids. Nothing to it."

"Shut up. You know Mrs. Kline only raised fifty-thousand last year. Your speech was awesome. The event was awesome. The silent auction was genius. I even won something!"

"Won is a matter of perspective," I replied. "Let me guess, the beach glass necklace?"

"How did you know? But did you see that thing? It was gorgeous. I think *The Glass Mermaid*, Kate, donated that. I love her shop."

I nodded but got side-tracked when Professor Lane emerged from the tent, her arms already outstretched, her velvet cape with its swinging tassels hanging like bat wings from her arms. Before either Viola or I could say another word, she'd crushed us into a bear hug.

"Horatio! Viola! Your mother would be so proud. You fully funded the summer theater program. I don't know how I can ever thank you," she gushed.

"Can't. Breathe," Viola whispered.

"Oh, Viola, you were always too dramatic," Professor Lane, who'd been one of my mother's dearest theater friends, said.

Viola opened her mouth to protest but just laughed instead.

"I need to head over to the theater," Professor Lane said, kissing us both on both cheeks as she spoke. The heavy scent of vanilla perfume swept off her. "We have *Sleepy Hollow* this weekend, you know."

"I have tickets for Saturday night," Viola told her reassuringly.

"Horatio. I want to talk to you about the renaming ceremony," she said then, taking me firmly by the arms. I stared into those same blue eyes I'd been looking at since I was a kid. Just being around her reminded me of Mom, and nothing could have made me feel better at that moment. "You need to arrange the event. This morning was fabulous. It's your calling, dear. That speech. I wept. Say yes."

"I'd really love to, but my father has me so busy—"

"Pshh," Professor Lane said, waving her hand to dismiss the idea that I actually already had a job, and my father, the land baron of Chancellor, as Viola and I called him behind his back, was not the kind of boss you wanted to displease—nor the kind of father. "Tell him you're doing it for Eleonora. He'll keep quiet. Wonderful job this morning," she said again, pinching my cheek with her jeweled fingers. "You know, the Chancellor Arts Council is looking for a new Executive Director. Just a thought. Bye, loves," she called then headed off, her dyed-red hair, practically cherry-colored, shining in the sun.

"There is no way Dad will let me work on another event. Not with Falling Waters about to open." The massive Hunter empire was about to take on yet another venture, an upscale restaurant located at a converted— well, partly-converted—location downtown. Dad had insisted I work with him on the project, even though I also seemed to be failing him at every turn.

"It's for Mom," Viola said softly.

The Chancellor Theater was soon to be renamed in memorial as The Eleonora Hunter Playhouse. My mother had spent her life devoted to that theater, raising money, directing plays, running theater camps, sewing costumes, everything...and Viola and I had done most of it alongside her. The Executive Director position, about which several of the board members had already approached me, sounded like a dream job. And it was...a pipe dream. Dad had me screwed down so tight with the winery, and the new restaurant, that I'd never get loose. I sighed. Losing Mom to cancer earlier that year had hit everyone hard. The theater had lost their most devoted patron, and we'd lost our most devoted parent.

"Yeah, you're right. I'll do it for Mom. To hell with what Dad thinks."

julie

An hour later, my car glided into the little lakeside village of Chancellor. I was right. It was harvest festival. The town was brimming with people. The streets around the main square had been blocked off for the festivities. I drove up and down the narrow side streets, many of which were bumpy cobblestone, before I found a parking place five blocks from Magnolia Lane.

I opened the trunk, grabbed the signs, and headed down the street.

Chancellor was a quaint little village. The small liberal arts college sat like a multi-turreted castle above the town, looking down on the town and lake. The land all around Chancellor, however, was surrounded with vineyards. The scent of grapes was in the air. The breeze—today at least—was also perfumed with the sweet scents of kettle corn, fried dough, wine, and pumpkin spice. Every parking meter was bedecked with scarecrows, corn stalks, and pumpkins. They'd strung garlands of witches' hats from lamp post to lamp post, crisscrossing the street. A band was rehearsing "Witchy Woman" on a stage nearby. Kids dressed in Halloween costumes—though the actual holiday was still a few days away—ran around, plastic pumpkins brimming with candy. Food vendors, craft vendors, trade demonstrations, and other attractions lined the streets.

As I walked down Main Street, dodging around princesses, pirates, superheroes, and even dogs dressed in costumes, I passed a large white tent adjacent to a wooded park. A sign noting "America's Best Ice Wine Challenge" hung over the entrance. Signs for Blushing Grape Vineyards were plastered everywhere. Inside, I saw people dressed to the hilt sipping wine from slim glasses. I veered out of the way when a horse-drawn wagon full of laughing children passed by, trying not to tromp on the groups of college students who were sitting on the street working on chalk paintings. I paused to look at a few of them. The designs featured Chancellor scenes: the lake, the vineyards, the college, but I also saw some of the students drawing mermaids, witches, and faeries. Chancellor was definitely turning out to be more interesting than I expected. We hadn't visited the little town often, but one year Mom and I had come during the Christmas season to visit their Yuletide Christmas bazaar and watched *The Nutcracker* at the local theater. I remembered sipping hot chocolate and watching people ice skate at the makeshift skating rink near the town center. It was one of the few times I remembered my mother looking truly happy. Most of the time she just looked harried. The ballet, however, was what had left an impression on me... but not in the way you'd expect. The next morning I woke up determined to make sugar plum pudding. I still remembered how good the house smelled as I prepared the dish. I remembered Chancellor being fun, and it still was. The quaint little town's energy was so alive.

For just a moment, I stopped to watch a gorgeous candle maker with shoulder-length curly blond hair dip a long taper into a vat of wax. He glanced at the crowd as he explained the candle making process. When he spotted me, he winked. He was around the same age as me and wore a pair of jeans that were ripped at the knees and a red and black flannel shirt. Shelves lined with jars of organic honey, beeswax candles, and lip balm sat at one side of his display. I smiled at him. He replied by tipping his head toward me. Then I headed down the street. To my surprise, I was actually close to the property. I caught sight of the sign for Magnolia Lane just over the roof of a vendor tent. Ducking under ropes, and shimmying between two tents, I finally stumbled upon Serendipity Gardens.

The little Tudor cottage, with pale yellow stucco siding, dark timbers, and a massive stone chimney near the large front window, sat tucked just off Main Street at the corner of Main and Magnolia. I propped the signs against the broken down fence and lifted the handle on the worn white picket fence gate. The yard was covered with knee-high goldenrods, purple asters, black-eyed Susans, Queen Anne's lace, and other wildflowers. I gently pushed open the gate and approached the house. It was a charming fairy tale style place, but it showed its age and disuse. The windows were shuttered, the window boxes overgrown. There was a small porch on the front of the house, but its crumbling roof was in need of repair. To the right side of the little house was a charming Victorian-style greenhouse that appeared to be attached to the building. Several of the glass panes were broken, and it looked like a jungle was growing inside.

I stepped onto the porch carefully, the old wood groaning as it took my weight. The green paint on the door was flaking off in chunks. Leaning along the side of the house was an old sign that read *Serendipity Gardens*. Reaching into my purse, I pulled out a wrought-iron key. It was then that I realized the top of the key was shaped like a heart. A faded red ribbon had been tied to it. I grabbed the door handle and was surprised to find that it was, in fact, a glass doorknob. It shimmered with amethyst color.

I slipped the key into the lock and turned it. Pushing the door open, I went inside.

The place was adorned with old baskets, hand-painted watering cans, and had an antique cash register sitting on the counter. Overhead was a chandelier trimmed with multi-colored beads. The vaulted ceiling, with its massive beams, had been painted to look like a forest canopy. Sunlight glimmered in and caught the light on the dusty chandelier, casting blobs of colored light all around the room. The image was breathtaking. The little place was simply...divine. Perfect. Dusty tables dotted the room. Clearly, they'd once been display tables. An old baker's rack sat in one corner. At the end of the counter was a beveled glass bakery display case. While it was covered in an inch of grime, it was truly quaint. Along the wall sat an armoire. Its lavender-colored paint had faded and worn off, giving it a shabby chic appearance.

Just to the side of the armoire was a set of double glass doors leading to the overgrown greenhouse. I peered through the glass and looked inside. Ivy was trying to take over the place. A vibrant-colored indigo bunting fluttered in through one of the broken panes and back out. A russet-colored butterfly flitted through the space like a fey thing, owner of a forgotten kingdom.

I was in love.

I slid my finger along the dusty shelving as I headed toward the cash register. The place was filled with so much character, so much potential. Who in their right mind would turn it into something as bland as a college administrative building?

I moved behind the counter, pushing aside the faded cherry-print fabric separating the shopfront from the back room. Immediately, I walked into a kitchen. It was a perfect 1950s style kitchen. It looked like it had come straight from the set of the *I Love Lucy* show. There was a refrigerator, a massive old-fashioned stove large enough to hold ten pies, a pot-bellied wood stove, and deep, cast iron sink. In the center of the space was a butcher table. The space could be turned into anything: a pizza joint, a café, a restaurant. The possibilities were endless. Serendipity Gardens indeed! *Who had*, I wondered then, *Mrs. Aster been?*

In the back of the kitchen was another door. I opened it, expecting to find a closet, but instead found myself standing in a small living room. The space, much like the rest of the building, looked as if time had frozen there in 1950. A pea-green couch and the smallest TV I'd ever seen—which had probably aired the moon walk—decorated the space. Just off the living room was a tiny bathroom, complete with a claw-footed bathtub. A second door led to an empty second room large enough to hold a full-size bed. I looked back across the small living space. It was perfect. Light shone into the room from a window. It cast its glow on the only photograph hanging in the space. I lifted the black and white photo off the wall and dusted it off. There, I saw five laughing women sitting around a table. They all wore flowers on their lapels, and every one of them was wearing a black witch's hat. Underneath the picture was written *Halloween Dance* and the names Alberta Pearl, Tootie Row, Violet McClellan, Betty Chanteuse, and Emma Jane Aster. I stared at Mrs. Aster, who was laughing so loudly her eyes had squinted shut. She looked...joyful.

Placing the photograph on the wall, I headed back to the storefront. I was about to start digging in my purse for my phone when I saw something...odd. The door on the lavender-colored shabby chic armoire was open. It had definitely been closed when I'd passed through the room. I remembered admiring the hand-painted designs on the doors.

"Hello?" I called to the empty space.

A soft breeze fluttered in from under the greenhouse door, causing the armoire door to swing open even further.

I crossed the room to close it but then spotted something shimmering inside, the sunlight pouring in from overhead glinting on...something.

The dusty armoire was empty save a small box tucked away in one corner. It had been painted silver and purple. I pulled it out. The box was small, wooden, and a figure of a woman with flowing hair blowing dust from her palm had been painted on the lid.

Curiosity getting the better of me, I opened the box. Inside, I found yellowed card after yellowed card of recipes. A recipe box? Recipes for lemon meringue pie, petit fours, dandelion wine, and so many other culinary delights were stuffed into the tiny box. Grinning like a Cheshire cat, I pulled out my phone.

I dialed Dad's number, but he didn't pick up. I let the phone go to voicemail.

"Dad, I'm at the property in Chancellor. We have a buyer...me. Let's talk when I get home. I'm not going back to school. I hate it. I...I want this place. I have an idea. Love you."

I gazed across the shop. The possibilities were limitless, but the one thing that needed to be there was me. My heart felt it with more certainty than anything I'd felt since Mom had died. I needed that neglected place as much as it needed me. What we would do together, I wasn't sure quite yet, but that was nothing a pumpkin spice latte couldn't remedy. Still cradling the antique recipe box, I snatched up the key and headed toward the door. But first, I needed to toss those signs back in the trunk of my car. They wouldn't be needed. And for the first time in months, that massive pain in my chest felt like it had melted away.

horatio

"Did you hear back yet?" my dad asked the moment I stepped into the ice wine competition tent. He was leaning against the bar right inside the entrance.

Despite the fact that I'd just run a massive charity event, and despite the fact that Blushing Grape's ice wine, Frozen Kisses, was in fierce competition for the best ice wine in the United States, all my father seemed to care about was his expanding empire. His focus seemed to be completely wrapped up in Falling Waters to the exclusion of everything—and everyone—else. The renovations on the wine bar and upscale restaurant were moving along well except for two snags. First, the town didn't want to give up The Grove, a public park by the old mill, so Dad could turn it into a wine garden. And second, the least important piece of the puzzle—which was why he had, of course, given it to me—was to acquire space for parking. No matter how many times I called Dayton Real Estate, I couldn't get a call back about the little hovel at the corner of Main and Magnolia that Dad wanted to level to build his parking lot. Though it was a tiny piece in the big picture, it scratched on my father's nerves...and me along with it.

"I was tied up with the charity event this morning. I thought I'd try again after the judging."

"For the love of—" my father said, setting down his wine goblet with such force I'd thought it would break. "Horatio, sometimes I wonder if you're even my son. It's such a small thing. Are you so incompetent? Call now. And if you can't get him on the phone, drive to the office. God, Judy could have handled this better," he said, referring to his secretary. He pinched the brow of his nose, squinting his eyes in irritation.

The bartender looked away, pretending he hadn't just seen a twenty-five-year-old man berated by his father in public.

Nothing was ever good enough for Dad. Nothing. And now that Mom was gone, his temper and impatience were worse than ever. He hadn't even asked about the charity event. My achievements meant nothing to him. The only thing that mattered was what he wanted. It had always been like that...grades, sports, college. Everything had to be as he liked it, and if it wasn't, he either didn't care or hated you for it. Anything or anyone who failed to meet his standards was just...worthless. And at the moment, that included me.

"Fine," I said and left the tent. Yanking my tie loose and pulling off my coat, I headed out onto the crowded street. The harvest festival was in full swing. Around me, people were laughing and having fun. Dad had managed, however, to sweep away my happiness with just a few words. My success was superseded by the urgency of a parking lot. At that moment, I missed Mom terribly.

Among the vendors, I spotted Rayne, my friend and unreformable hippie, who owned a honey farm at the edge of town. He was giving a demonstration on candle making.

"Is that the same kind of wax you have in your ears?" a little boy, about six years of age, asked Rayne. The boy was rolling a ball of warm wax around the palm of his hand.

"Not quite," Rayne said with a grin, looking up at me. "Ear wax is made up from your dead skin cells, fat, and other gross stuff," he said with a laugh as the boy grimaced. "This is made from beeswax."

"Bees... Like the kind that sting you?"

"And make honey. And these candles actually take

dust and allergens, the bad stuff, out of the air. Burn it up. They make you healthier...and they smell good."

"Cool!" the boy said then smiled up at his mother. "Can we get one?"

With a nod, the woman slipped Rayne a five for one of his beeswax candles then directed her boy on his way while he clutched his candle.

I grinned at Rayne. "Did you just make five bucks on that ten cent candle?"

"Of course not," Rayne said, stretching back to put his hands behind his head. "She paid me four-ninety for the education and ten cents for the candle."

"Ah, and here I thought maybe it was that twinkle in your eyes she was paying for." It had almost become a cliché. Whenever we went out, the girls always flocked to Rayne and his twinkly glow. But whenever they heard my last name, they immediately forgot his inner magnetism. Money twinkles a lot brighter than charm, not that it did me any good. What use was a woman who only wanted me because my last name was Hunter? It seemed nearly impossible to find someone sweet, authentic, and motivated by something other than my inheritance.

Rayne laughed. "How goes the wine business?"

"Pave paradise, that's my mission today. If I fail, I'll be cast out of the family."

"I thought you spent the morning digging in people's pockets."

"I did, and I did it very well, not that it matters. Half the socialites in there are already tanked thanks to my fine ability to organize canapes, drinks, and flowers. But it matters not to Mi'Lord Hunter. I'm headed over to Sweet Water to see if I can find someone to sell me that hovel on Magnolia."

"That place?" Rayne asked, looking over his shoulder.

I nodded. From the space between the tents we could just make out the forgotten nursery on the corner of Main and Magnolia.

"Why don't you just go ask the agent?"

"I've been trying to get the guy on the phone all week. No answer. I need to drive over to the office and try to catch him. And apparently, I need to do it right now."

Rayne shook his head. "The fey, my friend, have smiled on you this auspicious day. A very fetching lass toting property signs just went inside."

"What, now?"

"Like an hour ago. Hot, too. Red dreads, all peaches and cream. Lace up boots. Lots of bracelets. Definitely my type. Caught her with my twinkle for a moment, but she dodged me."

"Then by all means, let's go meet her. Get that

twinkle ready, because I need to leave that place with a signed contract, or I'll be cast off with you serfs."

"Well, I'll do what I can to keep you above the rabble," he said then leaned forward and put a lid on the flame keeping his wax melted and hot. "Hey Kate?" he then called to the vendor tent next to him.

I followed his gaze to the little white tent. Kate, the owner of The Glass Mermaid, whose necklace Viola bid God knows what to win, poked her head around the corner of the tent and smiled at us. "Hey Rayne. Horatio. Heard the charity event went well. Congratulations."

"Thanks, Kate. My sister won your necklace."

"I love that. I'll make her some earrings to match it. You need something, Rayne?"

"I'll be back in twenty. Keep an eye on my booth? I'll cover the wax, but it's hot. And, you know, the bees," he said, referring to the glass display holding a live beehive, "but they'll behave, won't you," Rayne said to the bees, gently tapping on the glass.

Kate nodded. "Got it."

"Thank you again for the donation," I called to her.

"Of course!" she said then turned back to her customers. From the looks of it, everyone was in the mood to buy beach glass jewelry today.

"She's smokin'," I whispered under my breath as Rayne and I headed toward the little house.

"Yeah. Married though."

"Too bad."

"Well, there's always more fish in the sea," Rayne said then laughed to himself.

As we turned the corner around the back of the tents, I took one look back toward the ice wine tent. From inside, I could hear the judge announcing the winners. Did they say we'd placed second...second? As my mind tumbled over the impossibility that Frozen Kisses hadn't won first, and the dire consequences it would bring on everyone in our business, I was completely lost. A split second later, I slammed into something and nearly tumbled to my feet, barely catching myself against a parking meter before I fell face forward onto the street.

"You okay?" Rayne asked. "I think you're bleeding."

I was about to answer when I heard a female voice reply. "I'm okay. Got my finger though."

Rayne had bent down and was helping up the most beautiful girl I'd ever seen. Her red hair flowed down her back, a pile of real estate signs were heaped at her feet, and she was nursing a cut in her thumb—an injury that, clearly, I had caused.

Great. What a wonderful day this was turning out to be. And thanks to my dumb luck, I'd just made the worst first impression on the one person I'd needed the most.

julie

"I'm so sorry," the guy who crashed into me said, his handsome face crinkling with worry. He had black hair and eyes the color of the sky on a bright spring day. Unlike his friend, the candlemaker I'd seen earlier who looked a little like someone from my drumming circle, the gorgeous guy who'd slammed into me was dressed in what looked like an Armani suit. The scent of expensive cologne, a sweet mix of lemon verbena and something soft, like an ocean breeze, effervesced off him. As he reached out, albeit tentatively, to steady me, his watch—which was platinum—glinted in the sunlight. He was undeniably handsome in a very classic way. My heart skipped a beat.

"It's okay," I told him reassuringly. "It was just an accident," I said then quickly turned my attention away, not wanting him to see the blush that had risen in my pale-colored cheeks. On my peaches and cream complexion, any blush was painfully obvious. No doubt this guy was used to having women fawn all over him. Sure, he was cute, and rich, by the looks of it, but it was the expression of concern on his face that got my attention. Trying to hide my obvious attraction, I turned to his blond-haired friend. "Thank you," I said as I righted myself. I dug into my bag and pulled out a tissue. The thumb on my right finger was bleeding like a gusher.

"Can I help you carry these?" the dark-haired guy asked. "It's the least I can do."

"Um, sure, thank you," I said nervously as I wound a tissue around my finger. "I mean, you don't have to...I was just going to take them back to my car."

"Oh," the dark-haired guy replied, looking confused. "I thought maybe you were putting them out. The property is for sale, right? I actually want to talk—"

"No, not anymore," I replied. I looked back at Serendipity Gardens. No, definitely not anymore.

"I'm Rayne," the blond said.

"Julie," I told him with a smile. Were his eyes twinkling? Like, actually twinkling? I'd never seen green eyes like his before. They were...enchanting.

"Which way to your car?" Rayne asked.

"Up about five blocks," I said then turned and started to lead the way.

"I'm Horatio," the dark-haired guy introduced himself. "Horatio Hunter."

That explained the suit. The Hunters were the most well-known family in Chancellor. Blushing Grape Vineyards, which belonged to the family, was practically a household name—at least in our area. "So that must be your event," I said, motioning to the ice wine event as we passed the tent.

"Well, my family's. Julie, right? Julie, I'd actually come over to talk to you about the property on Magnolia. We'd love to purchase the place. My father called your office but couldn't reach anyone. Maybe we can set up a meeting? If you have another buyer, well, we can certainly give a better offer," he said confidently.

My heart skipped a beat as I felt a flash of panic. Serendipity Gardens was just what I needed. I needed a new lease on life. But if the Hunter family wanted the property, my Dad might not be able to say no, especially if the offer was too high.

"I...I can pass your card on to my dad. He's the owner. But, like I said, I don't think the property is for sale anymore."

For a moment, I noticed Horatio's face twist with an

awkward emotion. Was that frustration or something else? I wasn't sure.

"You here for the festival too?" Rayne asked cheerfully, clearly trying to turn the conversation.

"Only incidentally. I'd come over to check on the property."

"I always liked that little cottage...it has a unique charm to it, don't you think? Why don't you stick around awhile? It's a great event. Horatio, take Julie down to Alice's. Our friend owns a bagel shop on Main. I bet she could fix her up with a bandage, and I'm pretty sure you owe Julie a cup of coffee."

"That's not necessary," I said as we reached my car. I had to protest a little, right? While the prospect of grabbing a coffee with Horatio was extremely enticing, I was already feeling antsy about getting Dad on the phone. I needed to hear from him that I could take the property. I needed to know that it was mine. After all, it wasn't really a business asset. We'd gotten it through inheritance. I just needed to get home and talk to him. Pulling out my keys, I popped open the trunk. "Thanks for carrying those. You really didn't have to. It was just an accident."

"My fault. I feel really horrible," he said as he loaded the signs into my trunk. "And I'd love to buy you a coffee...and a Band-Aid, if you're up for it."

"You're missing a great event. Speaking of which, I

need to get back to my booth. It was great meeting you, Julie," Rayne said, sticking out his hand.

Awkwardly, and with a giggle, I shook his hand left-handed, nursing my still-bleeding finger on my right hand. It was starting to throb. "Nice to meet you too."

With a smile, Rayne waved and headed back down the street.

I turned back to Horatio who had just finished loading the last of my signs back into the trunk of my bug.

"All set," he said, closing the trunk. "Ready?"

Horatio. Who in the world names their kid Horatio these days? "Really, you don't have to. I'm all right," I said.

"Are you sure? It's not every day I slam into the prettiest girl I've ever seen. Alice makes a mean bagel. If you're hungry, I'll spring for lunch too," he said with a smile.

I eyed him over. He really did seem sorry. And, considering my tissue was already soaked with blood, I really did need a bandage. And when I looked at him once more, peering into his light blue eyes, I liked what I saw. There was someone soft, maybe even kind, living inside those eyes. They intrigued me.

"All right, just let me stow this first," I said, setting the recipe box on the passenger seat of my car. As I set it down, I noticed what I had thought was silver paint on the lid actually looked like real silver. Someone had inlaid strands of silver onto the woman's hair, and the dust she was blowing seemed to be flecked gold. It was so lovely. I tossed a sweater over the box, just for safekeeping, then locked up the car. I turned back to Horatio who was unsnaking his tie from around his throat. I smiled at him. "Lead the way."

horatio

"Hey Alice," I called as I guided Julie, touching her gently on the small of her back, to the counter.

"Horatio? Here to blow some of that money you raised?"

I laughed. "You know that was for charity."

"Don't I count?"

"Only if you're going to run a bagel-making workshop for kids."

"You know, that's a cool idea," Alice said with a thoughtful grin.

"First, med triage. Got a first aid kit? This is Julie, and I'm pretty much responsible for slicing her finger open."

"Smooth," Alice said then turned to Julie. "Hi Julie,

I'm Alice. Want to come around back? I can clean you up," Alice said as she looked over Julie's finger.

"I don't want to trouble you. You're so busy," Julie said, casting a glance around the deli.

"Cleaning up Horatio's messes is something I'm very good at," Alice said with a knowing wink. She was right. I *was* less than smooth at times, and figuring out how to unglue gold diggers was a skill I hadn't yet mastered. Alice, on the other hand, knew how to pull them off like the painful burrs they were.

"Uh, okay," Julie said, curiosity filling her voice, as she headed around the counter toward the back with Alice.

From a distance, I watched the two of them chatting while Alice bandaged Julie up. They laughed like old friends. The scene made me smile.

The bell above the door rang. A guy with two small kids entered. He ushered them to the small kids' corner then went to the counter.

"Hey Cooper," Alice called. "Be right there."

The guy waved to Alice then headed over to play with the kids. The two children, a boy and a girl, giggled wildly when their daddy sat down at the kids-sized table with them and began serving them invisible drinks. I smiled as I thought of Viola.

As if on cue, my phone vibrated. I pulled it out to find a message from my sister.

Second place for Frozen Kisses. Suppose we ought to stay in a hotel tonight? Viola wrote.

Another state might be better. I replied.

For the love...he must be losing his shit. He's acting... weird. His smile is wider than his face. He even started giving me shit because you didn't get that property yet. Better work it out before he has a coronary.

Giving you shit? Why? Tell him to back off.

Take your own advice.

No. Seriously. He doesn't need to take that out on you. It's on me.

I frowned at my phone. Why would Dad go after Viola for something she had nothing to do with? I didn't remember Dad ever acting like this when Mom was alive. Viola had always been his princess, and I had been his protégé. Now I was the land baron's whipping boy and Viola just "didn't take anything seriously."

It's all right. Just try to get the property. Viola wrote.

Trying.

Try harder.

"Here we go," Alice said, returning with Julie. "You guys want lunch?"

"It's on me," I told Julie.

"Oh, definitely take him up on it then. He's notoriously cheap," Alice said, using one of her many well-rehearsed lines that was sure to send the gold diggers screaming for the hills.

Julie laughed. "That's no problem. I'm a cheap date. I'm game if you still have time," she said then, smiling at me.

God, she was gorgeous. She looked like she'd stepped out of a Botticelli painting, stopped by Woodstock for a makeover, then landed before me to make me lose what little cool I had managed to acquire over the years.

"Yes. I do have time, I mean. A muffaletta for me. How about you, Julie?"

Julie quickly scanned the menu board above the counter. "Avocado and tempeh?"

"Veg?" Alice asked.

Julie nodded.

"All right. Just give me a few," she said then waved us toward a table. "Cooper!" she called then, turning to the dad. "How's my mermaid?"

"Hungry," the man replied with a laugh.

"All packed up," Alice said as she handed him a to-go bag.

"Is here okay?" Julie asked, drawing my attention back.

I nodded, stopping to pull out her chair for her.

I saw her raise an eyebrow, but she said nothing.

"So you're a vegetarian?" I asked, sitting down across from her at the small table.

Julie nodded. "For about six years. I don't try to be sanctimonious about it. It's just better for my body."

"I've tried a few times. Nine months was my longest stretch. Pepperoni pizza defeated me."

"Hot dogs and Slim Jims, that's what I crave. And I'm not sure they're even meat. But I still haven't given in."

"Maybe you miss MSG."

Julie laughed. "Maybe," she said as she smiled nicely at me. "So, you were at a charity event?"

I nodded. "The Chancellor Arts Council. I organized their fundraiser. It went really well."

"That's so cool. I thought you worked for the winery?"

"Yeah, well, the winery is my family's business. I sort of fell into it. My mother—she passed last year—was really active in the art community here. It left a soft spot in my heart, so I try to help out."

Julie smiled softly and lightly touched my hand as if to comfort me. "My mom died over the summer. I understand how hard it can be," she said, brushing my hand in a kind of careful caress once more then let me go.

"Sorry to hear that. How..."

"Cancer," Julie answered.

"Same here."

"My mom...we had a relative who left us the property on Magnolia. You'd mentioned the winery was interested. It wasn't a regular real estate acquisition. We...I...inherited it. I'm going to pull it off the market. I'll be opening up a shop there."

Panic spread from my head to my toes. I could already hear Dad bitching at me, and then at Viola, about how we were costing him his dream. What in the hell was I going to say now?

"Here you go," Alice said, setting down two red plastic baskets, the perfectly prepared sandwiches inside, sided, of course, by her homemade chips. She set down two glasses of water as well. "Want anything else? Coffee or anything?"

"No. Thank you," Julie replied politely. "These look fabulous. Thank you, Alice."

"You're very welcome," Alice replied, and with a wave, she headed back to the kitchen, pausing to flash me two thumbs-up signs behind Julie's back.

I lifted the sandwich and took a bite while I considered what to say next. How in the hell was I going to get her to give up the property? It was an inheritance.

"Oh my God, this thing is amazing," Julie said. "It's got some wild cream cheese on it. Is that dill? And fresh basil. Wow," Julie said, examining her sandwich before she took another bite.

"What were you thinking of doing with the property?" I asked.

"I'm a baker," Julie said confidently. "I was thinking sweets, all organic though, and a tea shop. Like an old apothecary."

"Really?" I asked as my mind twisted with what to say, to do, next.

Julie caught my apprehension but misread it. "You don't think people here would like that?"

Panic. I felt the muscles across my chest tighten.

"I...I'm not sure," I lied. People in Chancellor would love it. Besides Alice's bagels, there wasn't a real bake shop in town, and the older ladies in Chancellor would adore a tea shop. But if I told her that, well, then there would be no talking her out of the property. "If you want to open up a place in Chancellor, the old Pizzeria over on Maple, really close to the college, just became available. That family retired, and pizza is always a hit near a college."

Julie eyed me suspiciously then shrugged. "I don't know. The old place on Magnolia has so much character, you know?"

I did know, but I also knew how pissed off Dad was going to be if I didn't get that property. "Sat a long time though. The roof was looking pretty rough. Plumbing and wiring might be a problem. Could be tough, and expensive, to turn it around."

"It's just so adorable. I love its vibe. What were you thinking to do with the place?" Julie asked, and this time I heard an edge to her voice that wasn't there before.

"We're opening a restaurant quite near that spot. Maybe you noticed the old water wheel just down the block from you? I think Dad is looking for some overflow space," I said carefully.

"Restaurant overflow? Like an extra kitchen? Storage?"

"Well, no, not really."

"Oh," Julie said then, setting down her sandwich. "So, more like parking."

"The building is just too old. I'd hate to see you go into the property. It's just sat unused for so long."

Julie sat back in her seat and sipped her water. She had a mildly annoyed look on her face. "So your Dad was planning to demolish the place? For parking?"

"Well, it just looks like a wreck. Probably not worth saving, no offense to your relative. It's just been uninhabited for so long. Listen, the winery could offer you a really good price for the property."

"I'm not sure—"

Panicking, I added, "I know we'd offer you more than

enough to get you into a modern shop, some place you wouldn't have to renovate. Name your price."

"But the property belonged to a relative," Julie said, her eyebrows furrowing.

"True. But I'm sure that relative would love to see you succeed in business, not waste your money on new plumbing. There are a few cute places on Main to rent. I could introduce you—"

"No, that won't be necessary," she said then started digging through her purse. She pulled out a ten and set it on the table. "Thank you for the lunch." She rose and strung her purse bandolier style around her body. "And please thank Alice for the Band-Aid." She cast a glance at her finger. "I...I don't think we have anything more to discuss. And I really need to head back."

Crap. Crap, crap, crap. I'd let my Hunter side out, and once again, big money shot his mouth off. This time, however, I'd scared off someone truly lovely.

"Please don't go, Julie. Sorry...I...I had to ask. I didn't mean to pressure—"

"No worries," she said, flashing me what I recognized as a fake smile. "Nice to meet you, Horatio," she said then turned and exited the building, the bell above the door signaling her departure.

As she turned and headed down the street, I could see

the look of utter disgust, frustration, and maybe sadness, on her face.

"What happened?" Alice asked, coming up behind me. "She start pocket digging?"

I shook my head and boggled at the truth. "No. I did."

julie

I t was late afternoon by the time I got home. My stomach was growling loudly, my finger ached, and I was still agitated with Horatio Hunter. Dad wasn't home yet. I headed upstairs to the bathroom and started digging around for a first aid kit. Dad hadn't thrown away Mom's makeup and other beauty supplies yet. I opened her little travel kit and found everything I'd been searching for: alcohol, Band-Aids, and Neosporin. As I sat bandaging my finger, my eyes drifted to her drawer full of nail polishes, eyeshadows, and moisturizers. Mom and I were so different. It was no wonder we could never see eye to eye on anything. I would never forget the look on her face when I told her I wanted to pass on the scholarship I'd been awarded and go to culinary school.

"What are you talking about?" she said, glowering at

me over her cup of coffee one Saturday morning just after I'd graduated from high school.

"I just...I just don't think dentistry is right for me."

"Then get your MD or become a psychologist or a nurse or something. The future is in medicine, Julie. How many times have we been over this? You have a scholarship. You're going."

"But it's not my passion. I want to do something that makes me feel...fulfilled. Like you and real estate. College...it just feels wrong. I'm a great cook and an even better baker. Maybe I could open my own bakery or restaurant."

"The restaurant business is risky. Most restaurants fail in the first year. Do you know how much turnover those buildings get? Passions can cost you. Trust me. Pick something safe."

"But if I go to culinary school, study the business..."

Aggravated, Mom set down her cup with a thump, spilling black coffee over the lip of the mug. "Don't ruin your future chasing some worthless dream. It's decided. And I'm no longer having this conversation," she'd said, and with that, I knew there was no use in arguing. I'd spent the next two years in college bored out of my mind, studying hard in classes I loathed and whipping up new recipes on the weekend. I'd tried to talk to her the summer before my junior year, before we knew why she was sick all the time, but she wouldn't hear it. "Julie, I know what's best for you. Don't waste your time chasing stars. You'll thank me later."

Sometime in mid-June, she woke up in the middle of the night unable to breathe. It was then that we learned that she was in the advanced stages of cancer. She was gone just two weeks before fall semester started. Pushed forward by the momentum of everything, come August I found myself sitting in the classroom wondering why I was there—again. By October, I was failing. And as my student advisor told me, I was sure to lose my scholarship if I didn't "get my act together." Act was definitely the right word. Sighing, I closed the med kit, put it back in the drawer, and headed back downstairs.

My bag lay half-open on the chair. I dug into my bag, pulling out the little recipe box. Whether Horatio Hunter liked it or not, I was going to follow my dream. I was sick of people standing in my way. And I was even more frustrated with myself for letting Horatio in. His eyes had tricked me. I'd thought I'd seen someone kind behind those baby blues. In the end, he was just playing me to get what he wanted. Well, that wasn't going to happen.

I headed back to the kitchen, prepared the portabella and goat cheese pizza for Dad and myself, then pulled out a chair and started looking through the recipe cards. They had faded with age to a soft yellow color. There was an interesting smell on them, like the mixed scents of vanilla and lavender. Mrs. Aster had left a trove of recipes: cakes, cookies, herbal teas, you name it. I pulled out all the recipes for sweets. There were at least fifty of them in the box. I thumbed through until I found a recipe for *Make a Wish Cake.* Well, I was definitely making a wish tonight. I skimmed through the ingredients. We had everything in the house. On the back, however, I spotted something unusual on the card. There seemed to be some kind of poem written alongside the recipe.

To get your wish. Over the batter recite:
Round three times you'll see my way
Stir backward once protests away
Round three times more to receive
In one bite, they will believe.

I grinned. It seemed like Mrs. Aster was the superstitious type, or maybe she just had a good sense of humor. Suddenly, this distant relative was getting more interesting. I tapped the recipe card on the table. Chasing stars, Mom had called it. Well, tonight chasing stars seemed like a good way to go. I stuck the rest of the recipes back in the box and headed toward the fridge. Half an hour, and lots of molasses, flour, butter, lemon peel, and ground anise, later, the batter was ready. I mixed all the ingredients just as the instructions read, then pulled out the card, reciting the lines over the batter just as it said, my wooden spoon stirring in tandem.

Round three times you'll see my way
Stir backward once protests away
Round three times more to receive
In one bite, they will believe.

As I stirred, the sharp scents of butter, lemon, and anise-filled the kitchen with a heavenly aroma. And if I wasn't perfectly sure that such a thing was impossible, I thought, for just a moment, that the batter had glowed with a golden shimmer, a glittery swirl of air sweeping up from the bowl. Weird.

The batter ready, I poured it into a cake pan. I then whipped up a little lemon curd buttercream frosting and set it in the fridge to cool. Then I sat down at the table and began drawing up a business plan. Over the course of the day, the vision of what I wanted to do with the place had jelled in my mind: tearoom, organic bakery, apothecary and other all-natural supplies. I could just see the old-fashioned glass case lined with my cupcakes and other treats. I could see the shelves filled with bottles of organic face creams and lotions. I could imagine little café tables in the greenhouse with tiered serving plates for high tea snacks. And in the summer, I'd plant cutting gardens in the yard. I loved the picture so much, and saw it so vividly, I could barely contain myself.

When the oven timer rang, I set my pad aside and rose, pulling the pan out of the oven just as Dad opened the back door. He was juggling his laptop and briefcase along with groceries.

"Here," I said, setting the cake on the oven beside the pizza to cool. I rushed over to help him.

"Thanks," he said, sighing heavily with relief. He set his stuff on the table while I started unloading the bags of groceries and stashing everything in the fridge. He'd bought all my favorite breakfast items: fresh multi-grain bread, capers, cream cheese, red onion, and arugula...the perfect breakfast food. I also pulled out pumpkin spice coffee creamer and my favorite brand of coffee from the bag.

"How'd it go in Chancellor?" Dad asked absently.

"Good, actually. I left you a message. Did you get it?"

"Sorry, my ringer was turned off. Been swamped all day."

"I actually wanted to talk to you about the property."

"Uh-huh?" he mumbled, his mouth full of something.

"Well, the property is really adorable. It's got unique architecture. And it's not just a shop. There is a living space in the back. It's a mess, but it could be turned around. I was thinking," I began, but when I looked back, I saw that Dad was holding the notepad on which I'd written my business plan. He was holding it in one hand while he stood over the cake pan with a fork in his other hand.

"Dad!" I said with a laugh. "That's hot. I just pulled it out of the oven. And it still needs frosting."

My dad looked from the paper to me. "You want the property in Chancellor? For this?" he said, motioning to the notepad.

I nodded.

Dad took another bite of the cake then looked at the paper again.

"I was thinking...I want to refurbish the greenhouse and set the place up like an old-fashioned apothecary. I'd sell teas, herbs, essential oils, and have baked goods made from organic ingredients. I even thought I could turn the greenhouse into a little tea garden. The shop on the inside, the tea garden in the greenhouse. I'd serve high teas, even let people reserve the space for bridal showers, things like that. I could live in the back. I have money saved up. I can make it work. I know I can. I'm a good baker, and I have a head for business, you and mom taught me so much. The property is right on Main among a bunch of cool boutiques, restaurants, and cafés. It's a perfect fit."

"Green Earth Apothecary & SerendipiTEA Gardens," my dad read from the business plan.

"Yeah, Green Earth Apothecary...Gea, like a play on the Earth Goddess' name. And I thought I'd use Mrs. Aster's old business name, Serendipity Gardens, change it up a little and marry the two together."

"This is your wish?" my Dad asked, looking at the paper.

A chill went down my spine, and goosebumps rose on my skin. Wish? Dad took another bite of the cake as he looked at my business plan.

"It is," I whispered.

"Then, done!" he said, raising the fork triumphantly. "Now, let me get out of my monkey suit, and let's have some of that pizza! Wow, Jules, this cake is amazing... butter, lemon, and anise. Zap. Tastes fabulous. My daughter is the next Martha Stewart," he said then wandered off, taking his fork with him.

I crossed the room and picked up the recipe card: *Make a Wish Cake.* Surely, it had to be a coincidence, right?

CHAPTER 8

horatio

I left Alice's deli and headed back to the ice wine event tent feeling completely defeated. Not only did I not get the property, but I'd also scared away the most interesting prospect I'd come across in months. Julie Dayton...a boho Botticelli. At that moment, I hardly cared what Dad had to say. He could do his worst.

And, of course, that's exactly what he did.

Grabbing a glass of Merlot, I crossed the tent and took a seat across from my father.

"Well?" he demanded.

"The property isn't available anymore," I said, sipping the wine. While I know I should have been concentrating on the red hue that was rising up from Dad's neck and across his face, the only red I could think of was that of

Julie Dayton's hair. How in the world was I going to find a way to apologize to her? I'd acted like a complete ass.

"What do you mean the property isn't available anymore?" Dad's voice was icy as he glared at me across the luncheon table.

Viola, who'd been chatting with another winery owner, must have sensed a family dispute was about to erupt. She pulled out a chair and sat, strategically, between us. "And what are we arguing about?" she asked as she pushed her long, dark hair over her shoulder. She was smiling as she lifted her wine glass and toasted someone across the room. "The tension between you is practically palpable. Can you two at least try to act civil in front of everyone?" she said while smiling and waving.

"Once more, Horatio has managed to screw up something both simple but important," Dad said, jerking his tie roughly.

"Well, all I've heard all day today is what a fabulous event he organized on the beach this morning," Viola said as she pulled a tube of lipstick from her purse and freshened up her makeup. "Horatio pulled off a bloody miracle, Dad. He raised a ton of money for the arts council."

"But he still managed to lose the property. And where are we supposed to put the restaurant parking now?" he asked sharply.

Viola sighed heavily. "They can just park at the city

lot. It's just a few blocks up Main. We'll get the city to give us some valet spots. Think outside the box. You don't need to flatten everything—or everyone—just to get what you want."

Frustrated, he glared at Viola. "And what about you? Have you heard back from the city about The Grove? What have they said?"

"Same thing they always say," Viola replied then paused to wave at yet another grower. "Love Dew was amazing this year," she called to the owners of one of the California vineyards participating in the competition. "You aren't going to get that land. It's a historic site. Chancellor is very particular about that kind of thing. We won't have room for the outside wine garden, but our patrons will have a beautiful view of the park."

I smiled at my sister in admiration. She knew how to handle Dad. Her *I couldn't give a shit less about his hard-headed ways* attitude was one I needed to adopt. But it had always been like that. Viola was strong-willed and had a good sense of right and wrong. Even when we were kids she would correct Dad when he punished us unfairly. Now, she did her job at the winery the way she thought was right. Me, I was still Dad's lackey, forever trying to please him.

"Mr. Hunter, they're ready for you now," the event manager said, distracting Dad who was now glaring at both Viola and me. He rose and headed toward the stage. In a moment, he'd give his annual speech congratulating the winners.

"You need to pull an Elsa on that crap," my sister said, turning to me.

"What?" I raised an eyebrow at her.

"Dad...just *let it go*," she replied in song.

I laughed. "You know how it is."

"Seriously. Don't even think about it anymore. We'll just get valet spaces at the public lot. It will be cheaper anyway. I'll convince him tomorrow. Don't let him freak you out. You rocked that event this morning. Everything was perfect. You should be doing more of that kind of thing, not chasing some haggy old real estate agent all across town."

"Actually, she was...well, not a hag."

"Oh! Do tell," my sister said then, leaning closer to me, her interest now piqued.

"The agent...her dad owns the business. She was adorable, smart, funny, and I pressured her over the property so she ran away."

"Good job," Viola said with a half-laugh, half-sigh. "Don't worry, you'll meet ten more just as pretty tonight and will forget all about her."

I thought back for a minute about those long red dreadlocks, how she bit her lower lip nervously when I touched her back, and how polite and kind she'd been with Alice. I frowned.

"Oh, whoa," Viola said, looking more closely at me. "Like that kind of fabulous?"

Dad tapped a knife against his wine glass, silencing the room.

I nodded.

"Flowers and an apology in person. Tomorrow. Wow, Horatio finally saw someone he liked," my sister whispered in amazement.

"It was bound to happen eventually," I replied.

"Was it? I wasn't sure. I thought maybe you and Rayne were planning to be perpetual bachelors...or maybe a couple," she said then grinned wickedly.

"Shut up."

"Make me."

We giggled, but then fell silent as Dad launched into his speech.

"Mom would have been happy to see you've at least noticed someone," Viola whispered.

"Yeah, but now I have to fix it."

"Then fix it. Oh, and the theater committee called the office right after the event this morning. Professor Lane works fast. They want you to organize the renaming ceremony. You should do it."

"But Dad—"

"Screw Dad. You know you want this. Take care of the renaming then go for the job at the Chancellor Arts Council."

"Dad will disown me."

"You won't need him anymore. You'd be free of him, the vineyard, and everything else...free to be your own man. And you're totally going to hire me, right?"

I grinned at my sister. My heart pounded in my chest. There had never been any discussion of what I was supposed to do with my life. The vineyard was everything. We were Hunters. We'd take over the dynasty. But what if that wasn't, exactly, what I wanted? What if I had different passions?

My mind drifted back to my memory of Julie Dayton's face. For the first time in what seemed like years, I'd met a girl who was real, a girl who didn't seem a bit interested in my name, at least not until I'd used it to arm wrestle the property from her. Alice was right. I was a moron. I'd make it right first thing tomorrow. I'd make my mother proud. To hell with what my dad thought.

julie

I returned to Chancellor the next day with a trunk full of cleaning supplies and a heart filled with joy. Dad was going to settle all the paperwork to transfer the name on the property and get the gas and lights turned back on. My father amazed me. It was like he knew, he always knew, that I was chasing the wrong dream. That he stood behind me meant so much. I'd make him proud.

A woman on a mission, I wanted to have the shop turned around before Christmas. Chancellor was famous for their old-fashioned downtown Christmas bazaar. My little shop would be a perfect fit. That morning I'd stopped at the courthouse in Sweet Water and applied for my operators' license and registered with the Health Department, after spending half the night working online to make my lightning-strike of a dream into a reality. It was nearly noon, and I was officially registered as Green Earth Apothecary and SerendipiTEA Gardens. Before the day ended, I'd be making a phone call to the college to drop my classes. Enough was enough.

Maneuvering through the streets as workers cleaned up after the street fair from the day before, I parked my bug in the side parking lot and toted all my supplies around to the front door. There was a back door to the living space, but the old wrought iron key didn't work there. I'd have to add calling a locksmith to my to-do list.

When I stuck the old wrought iron key into the door, I was overcome with a happy feeling that made my whole chest swell with light. Nothing had felt this right in a long time. Kismet.

"Honey, I'm home," I called to the empty space when the door swung open. From inside the greenhouse, a bird chirped a happy little song in reply then fluttered out the open window.

Windows. Windows had to go on the to-do list as well. Speaking of which, I turned then and opened up all the windows, most of which were covered with grime. As I opened each one, I stopped to draw a little heart in the dust.

"Hello, new friend, I'm Julie," I whispered. "Nice to meet you."

How long had Mrs. Aster owned the little shop? I slid my finger along the dusty counter. Well, I had to start somewhere. Popping in my earbuds and calling up my favorite folk music playlist, I grabbed one of the many brooms stuffed in the old broom closet. I was surprised to see that the handle of the broom had leaves, flowers, and some really old looking swirls and other designs burned onto the curved handle. That someone had taken the time to lovingly decorate the wood moved me. Taking a deep breath, I leaned into the music and swaying, started sweeping what looked like thirty years of dust off the floor as a sweet breeze blew in through the open window from the lake just a few blocks away.

"EXCUSE ME," I FINALLY HEARD SOMEONE SAY along with a tap on my shoulder. From the tone of her voice, I could tell it was not the first time she'd said something.

I turned to find three elderly women looking at me like I'd grown horns.

"Oh, sorry," I said, pulling out my earbuds. "Had my

music turned up too loud and didn't hear you come in. Can I help you with something?"

The two women standing behind a sweet looking older lady wearing a red and white polka dot raincoat smiled at me.

"Maybe you can. We hope you can," she said with a smile, looking from me to the broom I was holding. "Well," she added then, "I haven't seen you in a very long time. Girls," she said then, motioning for the others to take a look at the broom I was holding.

The most petite of the three, wearing a giant pink hat, gasped audibly. "Who are you?" she asked me then.

"Sorry," I said then, wiping my hand on my dirty sweatshirt. "I'm Julie Dayton. I'm the new owner."

Again, all three women looked at me as if they were in shock.

"New owner?" their leader asked.

I smiled. Apparently, this was the town busybody committee. If I wanted to make a go in Chancellor, I would definitely need the Ladies' Auxiliary on my side.

I nodded. "Mrs. Aster was a distant relative of mine. She left me the property. I'm going to reopen the shop."

Across the room, one of the carved brooms fell out of the closet onto the floor with a loud clatter.

The three older women looked at one another then, after a moment, laughed out loud. They giggled until the third woman, dressed in a purple suit, wiped tears from her eyes.

"Oh, we're sorry. Julie, wasn't it? Mrs. Aster was a very good friend of ours. I'm Tootie Row," the woman in the raincoat introduced, sticking out her hand.

"Violet McClellan," the woman in the purple suit said, shaking my hand.

"Betty Chanteuse," the petite little woman introduced.

The names immediately rang a bell. "One minute," I said. Setting the broom aside, I rushed to the back living space. I returned a moment later with the old photograph. "This is you then, the three of you, with Mrs. Aster?"

"Well, I'll be," Tootie said then, looking down at the image. "Was that '65?" she asked the others.

They nodded.

"Oh, look at Alberta," Violet said softly, pointing to another woman in the photo. "Our other friend. She passed away a few years back."

"I'm so sorry," I said. "But I'm so pleased you stopped by. I was hoping someone could tell me about Mrs. Aster. She was a distant relative. I never knew her."

The three women looked at me, their eyes glimmering with excitement.

"We'd be happy to, Julie," Tootie said.

"So happy," Violet added.

"Indeed, indeed. What a miracle. Emma Jane's relation. Alberta and Emma Jane...they were part of our cov —" Betty started, but Tootie raised a hand, cutting her off.

"Not now," Tootie said then, shooting her friend a knowing but friendly look. "Julie needs to get settled in first. What do you need, dear? What can we help you with? We know everyone in Chancellor. We can help you with just about anything."

"Well, at the moment, I need a handyman."

"Oh! I know just the one!" Violet said with a grin. "I'll send someone over."

"What else, dear?" Tootie asked, but her words were lost when a cement truck, followed by two utility trucks, pulled up across the street.

We all turned to look. Across the street and half a block down was an old watermill that Horatio had mentioned. It looked like, even without Mrs. Aster's property flattened, the Hunters were proceeding with their restaurant.

"Ugh," Tootie spat. "The land baron is hard at work, I see."

"He petitioned the chamber for The Grove again. We'll need to be at the meeting Thursday night," Violet said.

"They tried to buy this property," I said then. "They wanted to turn it into a parking lot."

The three women gasped.

"No," Tootie said.

"Well, they tried. Horatio...he was inquiring."

"Oh, that poor boy," Betty said then, shaking her head.

"Poor? Why poor?" I hadn't meant for it to show, but an odd tremor resonated in my voice, revealing my concern.

Tootie, however, had heard. She smiled at me, took me by the arm, then led me to the window. Through the still-dirty glass, I saw a sleek white Mercedes park alongside the trucks. Horatio and an older man, apparently Horatio's father, got out.

"There he is, the slick devil," Tootie said, the other ladies crowding behind us. "And Horatio. He's such a sweet boy."

"Kind heart," Viola said.

"His mother's son," Betty added.

"She died just a year ago. We adored her, a true artist, a gem in this town. She ran the theater, even let the three of us dress up as extras in a play. Horatio and his sister, Viola, sweet children, are much like their mother. Too bad they were left to get along with the land baron."

"Here, Julie," Tootie said then, positioning me so I

could look out the window a bit better. "You can see better here. Look over there. You see that water wheel? There's an old story about the stream that powers that wheel. They say that a fairy enchanted the water, so if you kiss your true love by the water wheel, your love will last forever. Isn't that a sweet little story? Isn't it enough to make you fall in love?"

"Fall in love?" I asked, puzzled as I strained to look out the window at the unmoving wheel.

"Fall in love," the three ladies answered in unison. At the same moment, Horatio walked into my line of vision.

He turned and looked toward me.

Gasping, I stepped away. Great, just what I needed, for him to see me gawking. As I stepped back, however, my head felt dizzy. Too much cleaning. I cast a quick glance outside. To my surprise, Horatio had turned away from the restaurant and was crossing the street. *Oh no, I was a total mess.*

I looked from my rumpled and dirty clothes to the three women. They were smiling at me.

They turned then, nodded to one another, then Violet said, "Well, Julie, it was very nice to meet you. Will you be staying here from now on?"

"Yes. I think so." Why did my head feel so weird?

"Great! Well, we'll be sure to stop by and visit you again soon," Tootie said. "And we'll send all the right people your way. Don't worry, you'll feel at home in Chancellor in no time."

"Okay, sure. Sounds great. Thank you for stopping by."

Tootie smiled. "Anything you need, just call us!" she said, and with a wave, she and her friends headed back out onto the porch. I followed behind them just in time to find Horatio headed down the sidewalk toward the shop, a sheepish look on his face.

"Ladies," he said, smiling awkwardly.

"Good morning, Horatio! Lovely weather. You come to try to buy the shop from Julie again? You do know she's Mrs. Aster's relative," Tootie said.

I suddenly wished I hadn't divulged so much information. While it seemed like the three women had now officially adopted me as Mrs. Aster's kin, I had never even met the woman.

"Um, well, no...actually," he began, then turned to me, "I came to apologize."

"Oh, well, now that sounds like something a gentleman would do. I hear your father is after The Grove again," Violet said, motioning to the park across the street from the shop.

"Yeah, Viola mentioned it," he said as he rubbed the back of his neck nervously.

"Hum," Violet said, tapping her foot. "Well, he won't get far."

"Not if we have anything to say about it," Betty added. "Your father can't snatch up all of Chancellor's historic sites."

"Girls, girls," Tootie chided them. "Horatio and his father are not of the same mind, are you, dear boy?" she said, reaching out to jiggle his chin. "Tell your sister hello for us," she added, then grabbing her friends by the arms, she maneuvered them off the porch. Before she was out of earshot, she called back to me. "Nice to meet you, Julie! We'll be in touch."

"Nice to meet you too," I replied with a wave. I grinned at the three of them as they headed across the street to the small park. As they walked, they huddled together like football players plotting their next move. Suddenly, I wondered if Horatio and I were in their sights. I laughed, shook my head, and turned back to him.

"Julie, I wanted to come by to apologize. I think I acted like a jerk yesterday."

"You think?"

"No, I did. I wanted to say I was sorry. My dad puts a lot of pressure on me. But that doesn't matter. I was out of line. I wanted to make it up to you."

"Then make it up to me," I said with a grin.

Relaxing, Horatio smiled. "Any preferences?"

"Surprise me."

Horatio grinned. "Challenge accepted." He shot a glance back over his shoulder at the mill. "All right," he said then, "I need to get back, but I'm going to see you soon."

I smiled. "Then see me soon."

Horatio grinned, inclined his head, then turned and left.

Kismet once more. Why hadn't I come to Chancellor sooner?

CHAPTER 10

horatio

G rinning like a fool as I headed back from Julie's shop to Falling Waters, I plotted the right move. What would a girl like her appreciate? What would be the right way to make it up? An idea started to form in my head as I grabbed a hardhat and entered the old mill. Inside, workers were stringing electric lines, knocking down walls, and maneuvering a massive timber to support the wall on the side of the old water wheel.

"Where did you go?" Dad asked, sounding annoyed.

About fifty lies popped into my mind, but I was getting pretty sick of being fake. "Across the street to talk to Miss Dayton."

"So you let the property slip through your fingers because the new owner is pretty, did you?"

"No. And I didn't let anything slip through my fingers. I told you already, Miss Dayton inherited the property. It was a family matter, not a business matter."

"Everyone has a price. You didn't try hard enough."

"They weren't selling."

My dad shrugged as he leaned over the blueprints, his sharp eyes taking in the scope of the construction. "Larry, where is the stoneworker?" he called to the foreman.

"Out. His kid has the flu. Single dad."

"Fire him and get someone else."

Larry looked shocked. "He's the best mason around, Mr. Hunter. He'll be back in tomorrow for sure."

My dad frowned. "If he's not here by six tomorrow morning, hire someone else. And tell him to get a babysitter." My dad motioned for me to follow him as he turned and headed outside.

Behind us, I could hear the slew of names the workers called my father. And honestly, I didn't blame them. All our lives, our mother had sheltered us from Dad. He came home in time every night to tell us sweet dreams then would work all weekend at the office. Mom, on the other hand, would have Viola and me out playing in the vineyards or on set at the theater dressing up and acting in the background, learning lines to plays far beyond our understanding. No wonder Viola had become so good at playing the part of wine heiress. Very few people understood it was all an act, saw how she really felt under her well-made-up smiles and designer clothes. With Mom gone, we now took the brunt of Dad full-on. It was more than a sane—or decent or kind—person could handle.

"How is it coming, Billy?" my dad asked a worker outside.

"Well," the man said, pulling off his cap to wipe the sweat off his brow, "Fish and Wildlife folks were by and gave us the go-ahead."

"Good," my Dad said, then turned to go.

"Only problem is," the man continued, not realizing he'd been dismissed, "the part we need is delayed. The mold for the pins broke. Gonna take another week."

"Another week!" My father's face started to turn red, the angry blush creeping from the neck up.

"They have to remake the mold, Mister Hunter."

"Jesus Christ, why is everyone so incompetent? What have you men been doing? I told you we need this place open before Thanksgiving..." my dad started and then he just let it rip. His voice became fuzzy as I tuned him out. I gazed back across the street at the little shop.

Through the dusty window, I could just catch glimpses of Julie's red hair and light blue shirt. She was dancing inside the shop as she worked. I closed my eyes and caught the sound of her voice on the wind. It blew across the space like a chiming undertone, a sweet bell ringing under the gong of my father's voice.

"Horatio! Do you even hear me?"

I looked back at my dad who was red-faced and angry. "I told you to get in the car and head over to Sweet Water. Take the address from this man, and go see what you can do to get that part immediately."

The man he called Billy handed me a crumpled business card with a shaking hand. I also noticed he'd gone absolutely pale.

"I have a meeting with the theater this afternoon to begin planning for the renaming ceremony," I replied.

"I'm not worried about your pet projects."

"Pet projects? That's for Mom."

"You can just hire a caterer, Horatio. Call and cancel."

Ignoring him, I added, "And Billy just explained that the mold needed to be recast. That takes time. What should I do, go blow on the mold to make it dry faster?"

Billy laughed, but then hid his laughter behind his hand when my dad glared at him.

Dad shoved his car keys at me. "You'll find a way to make it work."

Shaking my head, I stuffed the keys in my pocket and turned to go.

"And Horatio, don't come back a failure again," my dad called after me.

As I walked back to the car, I thought about my mom. "Follow your bliss," she would tell Viola and me. "Follow your bliss. The grapes will grow without you."

I looked over at the shop once more, and suddenly I felt my resolve stiffen. Enough of this. Enough. If Julie could be brave, why couldn't I?

CHAPTER 11

julie

Later that afternoon, I heard a knock on the front door.

"Excuse me?" someone called.

I was in the living area opening windows and investigating my new oven. "Be right there," I called.

Dusting off my dirty apron, I came around the corner to find a well-dressed man in his late fifties eyeing the room skeptically. His well-pressed suit, cornflower blue tie, and silver hair exuded the air of money. Though I'd caught just a glimpse of him earlier that morning, it didn't take more than a second to realize that Mr. Hunter was paying me a visit.

"Are you Miss Dayton?" he asked.

"I am. Mister Hunter, I presume?" I replied, reaching out to shake his hand.

He smiled weakly then gave me a firm handshake. "Yes. Aaron Hunter. I understand my son spoke to you about my company's interest in this property?"

"Yes. I explained to Horatio that I inherited the property from my relative. I'm planning to reopen the shop."

"I understand," Mr. Hunter said then pulled out an envelope and handed it to me. "You see, the proximity of this shop to my new restaurant is very desirable. We had hoped to use the spot for parking. I will definitely make the sale worth your while," he said, then motioned to the envelope.

I opened the envelope. Inside, I found a check written out to me for the value of the property plus twenty thousand.

"More than enough for a young entrepreneur to rent a suitable shopfront closer to town square and stock her store without going into debt. There are several places along Main Street for rent. I know a number of property owners who would rent to you at a good price. I can make sure you get a deal."

I looked him over. Aside from the color of their eyes, he and Horatio looked nothing alike. The eye color was nearly the same, but the spirit behind those eyes was very different. Yet, as I fixed Mr. Hunter with my gaze, I caught a brief glimpse of deep sadness behind his hungry stare. For his wife?

I handed him the check. "No. Thank you."

The paper flapped in the air between us. He didn't take it.

"Miss Dayton, you're making a mistake. It's always difficult to get a new business off the ground. With the right support, you'll be able to make things go very well here in Chancellor, but starting off with...tension...is not a good way to begin. It is an especially poor way to begin when that tension is between yourself and a well-established business."

"Tension? I'm not tense. The lovely ladies who were by this morning didn't seem tense. In fact, the only person around here who seems tense is you. You can't buy me out of a property that belongs to my family. And last I checked, you can't even accuse me of witchcraft to take my lands," I said with a chuckle as I folded up the check and slid it into the lapel pocket of his suit. What I hoped he didn't notice, however, was how badly my hands were shaking. A fit of adrenaline had taken over my body. I was trembling with both fear and rage. My heart was slamming in my chest. "I don't have to sell you anything. Now, if you don't mind, I'm very busy," I said firmly.

"You're making a huge mistake," Mr. Hunter said then, his voice turning icy and hostile. He took a step closer toward me. "I have powerful connections. I'll bury this business before it even—"

"What the hell is going on here?" a voice interrupted from the doorway.

We both turned to see Horatio standing there. He was carrying a box full of cleaning supplies.

"I told you to go to Sweet Water. What are you doing here?" Mr. Hunter asked his son.

"I didn't go."

"What?"

"It didn't make sense. Me breathing down someone's neck to 'make a mold faster' was ridiculous. I didn't go."

"Maybe we should step outside," Mr. Hunter said then.

Horatio crossed the room and set the boxes on the counter.

"From the sounds of it, you need to step outside," he retorted. "What do you think you're doing? You're alone in this building with this young woman, raising your voice at her? What the hell, Dad?"

"Step outside," Mr. Hunter said through gritted teeth.

Horatio pulled off his suit jacket and tossed it on the box. "No," he said.

"Horatio, I swear to God, step outside right now, or I'll fire you."

"You don't have to. I quit."

"Quit?"

"Quit. Yes, I quit. I quit the business, quit dragging around behind you, watching you twist into some unrecognizable human being with no heart, no empathy. Mom...Mom would be so sad to see you like this. I can't stop you, but I won't stand by you. Now, I think Miss Dayton asked you to leave."

"That I did," I said firmly, motioning toward the door. I wanted to wrap my arms around Horatio and plaster a huge kiss on his lips. But before that, it was taking all my will not to deck Aaron Hunter in the nose.

Surprising us both, without another word, Mr. Hunter turned and stormed out the door, almost knocking down a little man walking down the sidewalk. The little man turned and watched Mr. Hunter go then turned and looked back at me.

"Looks like the grape baron's got his feathers ruffled. Are you Miss Dayton?" the little man asked.

"I am."

"Mrs. McClellan sent me. I'm here to check the plumbing, get the water turned back on. Okay If I have a look around?"

I laughed. "Of course. Thank you."

"Oh, my pleasure. Emma Jane Aster let me take her to a dance once...you know, after her husband died. She sure could waltz," the man said, starring off dreamily. "Well, I'll be in and out if you don't mind."

"Please. Thank you," I said, shaking my head.

I turned back and looked at Horatio who had pulled off his tie and the crisp white business shirt he'd been wearing, paring down to a white T-shirt over his dark jeans. As he pulled off his dress shirt, the T-shirt slipped up just a bit to reveal a tanned six-pack with a blush of dark hair just above his belt buckle. Given the scene I'd just witnessed, and the fact that my blood was thundering so loudly in my ears that I could barely stand it, my heart still pumping hard, something inside me groaned. I looked away, feeling a blush rise in my cheeks.

"So, with that matter out of the way, what do we work on first?" he asked.

I looked back to see him toying with a hammer.

My head screamed, *the bedroom, let's work on the bedroom,* but pulling myself together, I asked, "What just happened here? Did you just quit your job?"

"Since my mom died, my dad has turned into the biggest ass on the face of the planet. As of this morning, I'm done. Today, I'm your handyman. Tomorrow, I'll start my position as the Executive Director of the Chancellor Arts Council."

"Well, then," I said, stepping close to him, taking the hammer from his hand, "seems like I have you right where I want you."

Horatio smiled at me.

I wanted to kiss him. More than anything, I wanted to kiss him.

"What now?" he whispered, leaning in toward me.

My stomach shook with giant-sized butterflies. "Floorboards?" I said, my voice shaking.

"Floorboards?"

"In...in the...the kitchen," I stammered. "They need to be fixed."

Horatio smiled, touching my chin lightly with his curled finger, then he took the hammer back.

"Then I guess I better get to work," he said and headed toward the back, leaving me behind with my heart still pounding. But now, it was thumping out a new song.

horatio

"Anyone hungry?" Alice called from the door of Julie's shop late that night. Without waiting, she entered at once, uttering an "oooh!" as she gazed over the room. Grinning, Rayne entered behind her. Chancellor's matriarchs had truly adopted Julie. All day long, plumbers, carpenters, electricians, lawn care workers, and even a guy to measure the greenhouse windows, had been by. By that evening, Julie had running water, electricity, the gas turned back on, minor repairs taken care of, and thanks to me, much of the shopfront cleaned...as well as her loose floorboards repaired.

"I always wanted to see inside here. I even snuck a peek through the window once. It's beautiful," Alice said, admiring the place. "Julie! Hope you don't mind the impromptu welcome party."

"You have beer and food. You can always come in," Julie said with a laugh.

"I'm just freeloading. Does that count?" Rayne asked.

"In my books, yes."

"God, look at this woodwork. This place is amazing," Alice gushed once more.

"I love it," Julie said wistfully. "I feel like I'm riding some strange wave of fate, tossing me along toward a dream come true."

Rayne, a perpetual metaphysical guru, smiled at that. "Massive action leads to massive results."

"Ah, another Rayne-ism," I said jokingly.

"No, that's Tony Robbins."

We laughed.

"Picnic?" Alice asked.

"Well, the greenhouse is mostly cleared out now, and I have some candles we could light. There are some paint throws in the back. I'll go grab them," Julie said then darted toward the back.

"She is adorable," Alice said to me. "Do not screw it up...again."

"I'm trying."

"So I hear. Viola called. She said you quit the winery."

"Well, massive action leads to massive results," I said, grinning at Rayne.

Rayne winked. "What's next?"

"The Arts Council...I took the job."

"No. Freaking. Way. You did?" Alice said.

Rayne nodded approvingly.

"It was time. I needed to move to something good, something different."

"And something sweet," Alice said with a wink.

As if on cue, Julie appeared from behind the counter. Her clothes were dirty from the long day of work, her cheeks flushed red from exhaustion, but she looked perfectly beautiful. Everything in me wanted to just crush her against me and hold her, protect her. She was just a tiny sweet thing, but she was no wilting violet. The image of my father standing over her, his face shaking with rage while Julie stood her ground, struck me to the core. In that single moment, I hated my father more than I had ever hated him before. And I was also struck with awe of this girl who took no shit from him, not caring even a little about who he was. That day, I'd seen both of them very clearly, and it was very obvious whose side I wanted to be on.

"Here, let me help you," I said, crossing the room to take the bundle of paint throws from her.

Alice, Rayne, Julie, and I then went about setting the blankets out on the floor of the old greenhouse. A worker had hauled away a ton of weeds, old pots, and worn tables, to reveal that the floor of the greenhouse was actually set with stonework. Overhead, wrought iron, the white paint now mostly chipped away, curved beautifully. Being in the greenhouse was a little like being in an ornate Victorian birdcage.

"This place is so cool," Alice said as she helped spread out the cloths.

"I'm going to open a tearoom," Julie said. "I'm going to get café tables for this area. I'll offer daily high tea. Wait, that won't put me in competition with you, will it, Alice?" Julie said. A look crossed her face when it suddenly appeared she might be drawing business off a new friend. The look made me adore her all the more. This was no ruthless businesswoman. And someone with a heart like that belonged in Chancellor.

Alice shook her head. "I mostly get the college crowd, weekend brunch people, people on their way to work. Sandwiches, coffee, and bagels on the run. Different market. But if you ever want to cross-promote, I'm all ears."

"You got it."

Alice set out dinner, handing each of us a box. "Corned beef on an asiago cheese bagel for the carnivore," she said, handing me a box. "Jalapeno Swiss cheese bagel and turkey for me, and for the resident vegetarians, grilled portabella parmigiana on a rosemary Panini."

"And an alcoholic beverage," Rayne said, handing us

each a pumpkin wheat beer, "not made from grapes," he added with a smirk. "Shall we toast? To Julie's new venture?"

"How about to Mrs. Aster, who was kind enough to leave this place to my family?"

Rayne nodded.

"To Mrs. Aster," Julie called, hoisting her beer.

"To Mrs. Aster," we all added.

At that, a deep chill swept through the place, and along with it came the sweet scent of flowers. We all paused and looked at one another.

After a moment, Rayne laughed. "Looks like Emma Jane didn't want to miss the party," he said then lifted his beer. "And may our lives be ever serendipitous," he added.

I turned to Julie. "To serendipity," I said.

She smiled softly. "To serendipity."

julie

B y the time Alice and Rayne left, my head was in the clouds. I picked up the throws while Horatio dropped the bottles into a recycling bin. Things in Chancellor were moving forward with such speed that I hardly knew what to think. The property, the help from Mrs. Aster's old friends, Horatio, it was a lot to take in at once. All this time, finding a great guy had felt a bit like finding a proverbial needle in a haystack. It seemed that most of the guys at college had only one agenda in mind, and while I had my occasional dalliances, that wasn't the kind of guy I was looking for. My mom's and dad's relationship had always been loving and respectful. My dad was a gentleman, and he had treated my mother like a lady. I wanted what they'd had. Thus far, I hadn't found anyone who fit the bill. Horatio had made a horrendous first impression, but now I understood what had motivated him. Wanting to make your parents happy was a driving force I understood very well. It made you do stupid things.

"Julie," Horatio called from the greenhouse. "You aren't going to believe this. Come check it out."

Putting the throws aside, I walked through the shopfront toward the greenhouse only to be awestruck. There was silvery light shimmering all around the room.

"What is that?" I whispered, stepping down into the greenhouse. The large, and what I thought to be decorative, silver and crystal chandelier overhead was glowing with soft light. "I thought it was just ornamental."

"I saw the electrician in here today, but I thought he was working on the floor lights. I just happened to brush against that old switch when I took out the trash," Horatio said, motioning to a round knob on the wall.

I gazed from the light to him. He was smiling, face turned upward, at the light. It shone down on his dark hair, making his pale face and blue eyes glow with iridescence. Maybe it was the beer, or maybe the gratitude I felt, or maybe my admiration for him that he would leave a toxic situation like he had, but in that moment, I felt myself drawn to Horatio. Earlier, fight or flight was ruling me. Now, however, I wanted him. I just wanted him. It was no more complicated than that.

"Horatio," I said, taking his hand gently, "thank you so much for everything. I know that this place, well, it tore your life apart. I'm sorry that it happened because of me."

He shook his head as his hand drifted to my lower back. He pulled me closer. "It wasn't your fault. But I'm glad it happened. And glad I met you. Thank you for tearing my life apart."

I gazed deeply into his eyes. "My pleasure," I replied and leaned toward him.

Some first kisses are like duds. It's all anticipation, and then the delivery just falls flat...a peck, a tongue driving toward your esophagus, onion breath, too much or too little pressure. First kisses are tough. But this...this was just right. Horatio's lips were soft and warm. His mouth tasted sweet, the hint of pumpkin lingering on his tongue. We pressed our mouths together, kissing softly. First came the sweet touch-and-go kisses, but then we became more passionate, our bodies pressing against one another. I could feel how fit he was, his muscles firm under his thin T-shirt. His arms gripped my small frame, pulling me close. He was so strong.

"Am I seeing stars or is it just the twinkling lights?" Horatio asked with a laugh.

"Stars, of course," I whispered. "Chasing stars," I muttered absently as Horatio drizzled kisses down my neck. Since the moment I saw the photo of the little shop that's exactly what I'd been doing, chasing stars. And despite my mother's insistence that such acts were futile, I saw a lot to the contrary.

"Julie," he whispered in my ear. "I really like you. And I really want to stay, which tells me I really need to leave. You're not like anyone I've ever met before. I want to deserve you. I want you, and not for just one night. I want more than that from you. Does that make sense?"

"Yes," I whispered. I wanted him too. Badly. But I wasn't in it for a one night stand either. The Horatio who had stood up to his father was the kind of man I wanted in my life.

He kissed me on my forehead then we pressed our foreheads together. "You're staying here tonight?"

"Yes. I'm going to keep working."

"I'll stop by or text you. I'm not sure what kind of mess I'll need to clean up now. My sister...I need to make sure everything is okay with Viola. With Dad so pissed off...I just need to check on her."

In that moment, I couldn't have adored him more. "Okay. Thank you so much for today."

"Thank you too."

I giggled. "Made your life a mess."

"That's what bakers do, right? But the result is always sweet."

"I hope so."

"I know so. Good night, Julie Dayton," he said, then leaned in and kissed me once more.

"Do that again, and I'm not going to let you leave, no matter how chivalrous you're trying to be," I whispered once he let me go.

Horatio laughed.

I followed him to the door, grabbing just one more kiss before he bounded off the front porch toward his Mercedes SUV parked on the other side of the street. With a wave, he hopped in the vehicle and drove off.

I stepped onto the porch and looked out over the garden. I'd been so busy inside all day that I'd barely had a chance to see what had been uncovered in the front yard. I walked to the end of the porch and started down the steps toward the cutting garden. I was surprised to find massive white flowers growing all along that end of the porch. They looked up at the full moon. Night blooming flowers? How lovely.

The moon made the whole yard shimmer with silver and blue light. The workers had uncovered several raised beds that must have been used for herbs or cutting gardens. They'd already started replacing the old, rotted wood with fresh planks. It was then, however, I noticed that something unusual had been uncovered at the center of the space. Held aloft by three metal poles was a massive old cauldron. It had been completely overgrown, hidden by the foliage.

"Now, where did you come from?" I asked, spying down into the cauldron.

Apparently, it had collected some rainwater because when I looked inside, I was surprised to see my own face, framed by the starry sky, looking back at me. Startled, I gasped and stepped back, giggling at myself.

A cool wind swept across the garden, kicking up with it the sweet smell of flowers. I looked back into the cauldron again, and this time I was amazed. Reflected on the mirrored surface of the water wasn't my face, but that of Mrs. Aster.

"Welcome home," she whispered in a thin voice, smiling softly at me. But then it seemed she touched the surface of the water, distorting the image.

"Too much pumpkin beer, and meeting the guy of my dreams, and Halloween week are doing weird things to my mind. Goodnight, Mrs. Aster. Thank you very, very much for the home. I'm headed to bed before I spy the Great Pumpkin or something," I said then turned to go inside, my skin completely covered with goosebumps.

As I headed back inside, the brisk wind whipped across the garden once more, carrying with it the strong scent of jasmine and a soft whisper in the breeze that sounded like someone had said, *you're welcome*.

julie

That night, I slept on Mrs. Aster's old couch only to wake up to the sound of workmen on the roof. I definitely needed to figure out a way to thank Mrs. Row for everything she'd done for me. It was like the whole town had turned out to welcome me, for better or worse. So far, despite my visit from Aaron Hunter, it was turning out to be for better.

I rose groggily, grabbed my overnight bag, and headed to the bathroom. I dressed in my cutest denim overalls and got to work. Pulling my hair back in a twist, I washed up, stopped in the kitchen to make a quick cup of tea, then headed out on the front porch.

"Morning, Miss Dayton," someone called from the garden. I turned to find the lawn worker busily working on my garden boxes.

"Up so early?" I called.

"Oh, well, I'll get you all finished today so you can get some bulbs in before the first frost. Emma Jane always had the prettiest daffodils growing out here. You know, she let me take her to dinner once," the older man said with a wistful smile. "Lovely girl," he added then went back to his work.

Okay, now that was the second aged gentleman in Chancellor to wax poetic about Emma Jane. Those must have been some memories if they were lining up decades later to have a chance to show their gratitude. I giggled at the thought of it. Just when did Grandma Belle's brother Owen die that Emma Jane had so much time to date?

On the front porch was an old potting table. I moved it out to the front garden. Grabbing a bucket and hose, I scrubbed it clean. As I worked, I eyed the busy street. Mr. Hunter arrived at Falling Waters just as I finished cleaning off the table. He slid out of his white Mercedes like a slick fish swimming upriver. He paused and looked across the street toward me.

Grinning, I waved to him.

He turned and went inside.

I noticed then that several official-looking people were moving down the street toward the park called The Grove. What was going on?

Just then, however, a white pickup pulled up at the parking along Main Street in front of the shop.

"Are you Miss Dayton?" the man in the driver's seat asked. Three men were packed into the front of the pickup. I couldn't help but notice that the driver was an older gentleman. Yet another of Emma Jane's conquests?

"That's me," I called.

"I'm Milt, Mrs. Row's husband. Got my helpers here. Toot said Emma Jane's old place could use some paint. Got a favorite color?"

"I like Emma Jane's green," I said, motioning to the shutters. "Maybe something plum colored for inside?"

Milt nodded as his assistants got out of the truck. "I'll grab the paint. The boys will start priming the place up."

"But Mr. Row, I'm not sure I can affor—"

"We've got it, Miss Dayton," he said. He waved to his workers then headed off.

"Mind if we go inside?" the men asked, both of them carrying toolkits and paint cans.

"I guess not," I said with a grin.

I shook my head as I watched them go.

Grabbing the old sign for Serendipity Gardens that had been lying on the porch, I laid it down on the old table then headed back inside to bring the paints I'd brought with me. Cracking open a can of chartreuse-colored paint, I painted a base coat on the faded sign. The bright green base coat dried while I washed out my brushes. Now I was ready for the real trick. Grabbing the recipe box from inside, I headed back to the garden with black paint and a thin brush. On one end of the sign, I began painting the image of the woman with long hair just as she was depicted on the recipe box.

I worked for a long while, concentrating hard. I didn't look up until a shadow loomed over the sign, startling me.

"Is that...*the* recipe box," a woman said aghast.

I looked up to see Mrs. Row standing there. She had a shocked impression on her face.

"It was left...for me," I said, realizing the moment I said it that it was true. "Mrs. Row, I don't know how I can ever possibly thank you for everything you've done for me. And I have no idea how I'm going to repay you."

"The box...can you make the recipes? Have you...have you tried one? Can you do *it*?" The woman had an earnest expression on her face. It was then I realized what she was really asking. She wanted to know if I had tried one of the...poems. No, that wasn't the right word for what they were nor the effect they seemed to have. She wanted to know if I had tried one of the...spells.

"Yes."

Mrs. Row grinned. "There used to be a recipe for

these adorable little cupcakes with sugar forget-me-nots. Make me about five dozen of those, exactly as the recipe says, for the public hearing on The Grove tonight, and we'll call it even."

"Tonight?"

"Yes. At seven. Can you manage it?"

I pulled out my cell. It was only ten. I had time. "Sure. But all this? Just for some cupcakes?"

Mrs. Row laughed. "You're sure you have made something from that box before...and the recipe...*turned out*?"

I nodded.

"Then, yes. All that for some forget-me-not cupcakes. Don't be late. About five dozen delivered to the town hall tonight no later than seven. Promise me you'll do that, Julie?"

"Of course."

"That's a good girl. Better start baking," she said then, patting my arm. With a wave, she crossed the street to join the businessmen and women gathered in The Grove. I couldn't help but notice that Aaron Hunter had joined them as well. A young woman with long, dark hair was at his side. She was looking in my direction.

She waved to me. Was she Horatio's sister?

Smiling, I returned the gesture then dropped my paintbrush into a cup of water. If I was going to bake cupcakes, I'd need to get to work. First, I'd get cleaned up. Then, I needed to grab some supplies. This was the first order from my new business. I couldn't wait to get started.

Tucking the recipe box under my arm, I headed inside.

horatio

The Town Hall was packed. Against my better judgment, I went with Viola to the meeting regarding The Grove, mostly to offer her some moral support.

"They're going to shoot down his request. They've all but told him so already," she whispered to me.

"Then what in the hell is he doing here? The Grove is a town landmark. They aren't going to let him scoop up the property."

"He was on the phone with his accountant this morning," Viola whispered. "He's going to pull a godfather."

"A godfather?"

"Make them an offer they can't refuse."

"He's out of his mind. He's going to sink the winery just to open this restaurant. I don't understand. I mean, having a venue for the winery is nice, but the vineyard tours are doing fine. What is so important about Falling Waters? To sacrifice—"

"You. To sacrifice you. To sacrifice the relationship he has with the town officials. I don't know," Viola said then as she cast her eyes across the room. I watched as her eyes landed on Dad who was chatting up President White. "I don't know," she whispered more quietly, this time to herself.

"Cupcake?" I heard someone ask from behind me.

I turned to find Julie standing there. She was wearing a purple dress with an embroidered neckline and cowboy boots. I looked down at the tray she was holding. On it, she had neatly arranged delicate looking mini cupcakes, each topped with light blue icing and a small blue flower.

"Julie," I said with a smile then leaned in to give her a polite "in public" hug. "Meet my sister, Viola," I said then, turning to Viola who was already grinning at Julie.

"Nice to meet you," Viola said then. "Let me guess," she added, looking down at the cupcakes, "Mrs. Row?"

Julie smiled and nodded. The lines around her mouth quivered a little. Was she nervous to meet Viola? "She seems to have adopted me."

"Take it," Viola said, lifting one of the petite cupcakes from the tray. "Mrs. Row knows everyone. And more importantly, everyone likes her." Viola popped the cupcake into her mouth then sighed heavily. After a moment she asked. "What in the world? That was about the best bite I've ever had. What kind of cupcake is that?"

"Lavender cake and honey buttercream frosting. Rayne hooked me up."

"Eat this," Viola said, snagging one of the cupcakes and shoving it into my mouth.

She really didn't need to tell me that Julie's hands were talented and sweet. I'd had just the lightest of tastes the night before. But the second my sister squashed the petite little cupcake into my mouth, I was overcome. It was so...perfect. The earthy, slightly spicy, taste of the lavender mixed with hints of lemon and honey. The cupcake melted in my mouth the way Mom's pineapple upside down cake used to do. The cupcake's lavender flavor, melding with Rayne's honey, took me back. My head felt dizzy, and I was suddenly overcome with a memory of my mom and dad.

As if I were in a fog, I heard Mrs. Row call, "Everyone, please take a seat. We're about to get started. A new member of the chamber of commerce, Miss Julie Dayton, is circulating the room. Please try one of her confections. She'll be reopening Mrs. Aster's Serendipity Gardens. She has samples for everyone. Try a bite. Don't be shy. She's sworn she's taken out all the calories."

THOUGH I HEARD MRS. ROW'S WORDS, MY HEAD was flooded with memory. It was like I was sucked back in time. In my memory, Viola and I must have been around eight and six years old. We were walking behind my parents as we meandered down the street during the Christmas bazaar. We'd just come from *The Nutcracker* and were dressed in our theater finest. I remembered the cold wind whipping through the fabric of my fancy dress pants, and Viola begging to stop for hot spiced cider. The scent of roasted almonds, gingerbread, and cloves filled the air.

"Of course, my little love," Mom had told her, patting her gently on the head.

We turned and headed toward the cider stall, but my parents delayed for just a moment as we made our way, stopping on the sidewalk just outside the old, broken down mill. A shimmer of ice and snow glinted off the frozen water wheel.

My parents kissed.

Viola giggled.

"Eww," I said.

Dad laughed, stroked Mom's cheek gently, then

kissed her again. "Don't you know why I always kiss your mom at the water wheel?"

"Why?" Viola asked brightly.

"Because this is where I proposed to her. Right here is where your mom agreed to be my wife."

"The Water House, as the place was called back then," my mom said wistfully, "used to be a restaurant. We had dinner there, then your dad brought me out here and proposed."

"That's so cute," Viola gushed.

"Then we drank one of my first bottles of Blushing Grape ice wine in The Grove," Dad said, smiling.

"Special night," Mom whispered.

"The best night," my dad corrected. "And the best Christmas gift ever, until you two came along," he added, picking me up and putting me on his shoulders. "Now, I think I saw a candy cane about as tall as you over there. Up for a challenge?" he asked me, heading toward one of the vendor stalls.

"Of course!"

"That's my boy."

"HORATIO," VIOLA SAID THEN, SHAKING MY shoulder, "we need to do something. Say something," she added, and this time I heard the urgency in her voice.

"This town," my dad shouted, "you people. You're nothing but a bunch of ingrates! Ingrates! I should burn down the vineyard and see how long it takes before you all go out of business."

"Mr. Hunter," Mayor Cumberbatch said, looking pale, "we don't mean to offend you. It's just as Doctor Franklin and Mrs. Row shared, The Grove isn't just a green space, it's a historical landmark. When the witch trials reached Chancellor, it was at The Grove that the witches in this town—such as they were—came to an accord with the townspeople. Chancellor is unique among other early Puritan communities. The people of Chancellor embraced the skills these women had and honored their sacred space. The trees in The Grove—"

"Are just trees!" Dad shouted. "I'm offering you half a million dollars just to let me section off The Grove for an outdoor restaurant. I'm not going to cut down any trees. You're being ridiculous. This whole town is being—"

"Dad!" I called.

I looked around the room. Everyone was staring at my father in shock. My dad had always been a shrewd businessman, but this...this was something quite different.

My father turned and looked at me. His face was

ashen. I could see he was trembling.

But now, I understood.

I remembered.

He was doing this for Mom.

"Mister Hunter, the vote has been tallied. The community has voted overwhelmingly against you," the mayor told him firmly.

"We value history here," Mrs. Row told him. "We're sorry, but we cannot let you have The Grove."

I looked from Viola, who looked pale, to Julie, who had taken a seat behind us. Her eyes were welling with tears.

The room was silent.

My dad ran his fingers through his thinning hair, took a deep breath, then straightened his tie.

He then turned and walked down the aisle of the meeting room and out the front door, the wooden doors clattering shut behind him.

"Go after him," Julie leaned forward and whispered in my ear.

I looked back at her. She was right.

Viola turned to me.

"Vi?"

Viola nodded. "Go. I'll stay and try to save the family name."

With all eyes on me, I rose. "Excuse me, Mister

Mayor."

He nodded, understanding.

Turning on my heel, I headed outside into the night air. The fall air was bitter cold. It bit my cheeks the minute I stepped outside. It felt like it might snow. I scanned around and saw Dad walking down Main Street toward the restaurant.

"Dad?" I called, hurrying after him.

He didn't stop.

"Dad?" I called again.

I finally caught him and tried to take him gently by the arm.

Dad turned on me, tears streaming down his cheeks. His gaze was icy.

"You betrayed me," he whispered.

"This isn't about you and me. I know why you want The Grove. The Wheel. This is about Mom. I remembered the story...your proposal," I said.

Dad winced at the last part.

"Dad, Mom would never want you to—"

"What do you know? What do you know about any of this?" he said then, shrugging me off. "You abandoned me, Horatio. You abandoned me too," he said angrily then turned and headed back up the street.

I let him go. At last, I understood. Now I just needed to figure out how to make it right...for all of us.

CHAPTER 16

After Horatio and Aaron left, the room sat in stunned silence until Viola spoke.

"I...I apologize. My father's actions, words, don't represent all the shareholders at Blushing Grape. I think my father is...unwell this evening. You won't be hearing from us about The Grove any further. Please, Mister Mayor, feel free to carry on with the agenda," she said confidently.

Reassured by Viola's words, the mayor subtly redirected business. What most of them didn't see, however, was how Viola sat shaking in her seat.

"Are you okay?" I whispered, setting my hand on her shoulder.

She nodded. "I just...I'm okay," she said then pulled out her notepad and took notes for the next twenty minutes until the mayor called a break at which point she rose, shook hands with a few of the town leaders, then bolted out the door.

Without thinking twice, I headed out behind her.

"Viola?" I called.

She was digging in her purse for a tissue. She must have burst into tears the second she'd stepped outside. She stopped and dabbed her eyes, but she was shaking violently.

"It's okay," I said, wrapping my arm around her. "Come on. Let's walk a little, get you some air."

Viola exhaled deeply then we turned and walked.

"My whole family is falling apart. First my mom, now my dad is losing it, treating Horatio and me like garbage. I...I don't know what to do. Before my dad freaked, I remembered something my mom used to tell Horatio and me. 'Follow your bliss. The grapes will grow without you.' I've been so busy looking after Dad, after the business, I don't even know who I am anymore."

"Sometimes our world has to fall apart in order for us to really see ourselves."

Viola sighed heavily.

When we reached the little park called The Grove, we stopped.

"It's a pretty place. Have you checked it out?" Viola asked, sniffling a little.

I shook my head.

Steadying herself by gripping my shoulder, she reached down and pulled off her heels. "Come on. Shoes off," she said, leading me into the trees.

From my view across the street, I could see the little park was wooded, but it wasn't until I actually set foot among the trees that I realized that the tall trees had been planted in a circle. At the very center of the park was a reflecting pool. I could see the full moon overhead reflected in the water. The earth was cold under my feet, but the fallen leaves made a soft cushion. All around the reflecting pool were stumps of wood which served as seats. Careless about her designer suit, Viola sat down on the ground beside the water.

"It really is a beautiful place," I said, but more than that, I could feel the electricity in the air. The place, which had been special to the witches of Chancellor, felt really magical. And more and more, I was beginning to suspect what my place might be in the grand scheme of things.

"My mom would bring me here sometimes. We would sip ice wine, even before I was twenty-one, and just talk about life. Our ice wine is the only wine my parents ever brewed together. All those flavor tests. All those trial blends. Finally, on a cold winter night, they got it just right, and Frozen Kisses was born. Now, my dad is ripping everything apart. It's like he's lost sight of everything," she said then sighed heavily. "God, Julie, I'm so sorry. We just met, but I feel like I can really talk to you. Must be your vibe with my family. Horatio seems to feel the same way."

"Well, being fed up with life is something I understand well. As of last week, I had no idea what I was doing with my life, but I've found new purpose, my own purpose, for the very first time. My mother died over the summer. She wanted me to be a dentist. I wanted to be a baker. It wasn't until that," I said, pointing to the property across the street, "happened, that I decided it was okay to give up on my mother's dream and be my own person."

"Your dad...is he behind you?"

"My dad always understood me. Now that it's just him and me..."

Viola nodded and touched the surface of the reflecting pool. The water rippled. "I'm glad you came to Chancellor. Don't go anywhere anytime soon, okay?"

I laughed. "Seems I've been adopted here. I'm staying."

Viola rose, brushing leaves from her pants. "I need to go. I need to find Dad. He shouldn't be alone right now. Thank you, Julie."

I smiled, rose, and pulled her into a hug. "You're welcome."

"See you soon?" she said then let me go.

I nodded.

After she left, I sat down on one of the stumps and looked into the water. The reflection of the full moon was enchanting. It filled up the water in the pool almost completely. I took a deep breath and tried to get my mind to stop spinning. So much was happening so fast. Somehow I'd managed to get sucked into the heart of Chancellor before I'd even caught my footing, but it felt okay...almost right. It was like I was meant to be in this little town all along, like I'd been meant to take Mrs. Aster's old place, like I'd been meant to find the recipe box. But how? Why?

The sound of low voices and rustling grass caught my attention. I rose and turned to find Tootie, Violet, and Betty standing there.

"Oh good," Tootie said. "We won't even have to go across the street to fetch you for the induction after all. How'd you know to come here?"

"I didn't. Induction?"

"Of course," Viola answered. "After the charm you just cast over everyone tonight, we figured we'd better get your training started right away before your powers run rampant."

My mind boggled. "Powers? Training? What kind of training?"

It was then I realized that each of the three women were holding brooms. In fact, Tootie was carrying two. At the entrance of the park, I saw other figures moving toward The Grove. More women, many of whom I recognized from the meeting, had arrived carrying brooms.

"Julie! So nice to see you again," Dr. Franklin, a historian from the college who'd spoken about the history of The Grove, called. "Welcome to the sisterhood."

"Tootie, what's going on?" I asked.

"Emma Jane was always the best of us. Her spell work was divine. Those cupcakes you made...wow, more powerful than any Emma Jane had ever made. You had all of us calling up long-forgotten memories. You've got strong magic in you, Julie. Emma Jane chose her successor very well. Come now, my dear. Let's get you dedicated," she said then, holding out a broom toward me.

"To what?"

"To the sisterhood, of course. We are the witches of Chancellor, and this is our grove. Welcome, my dear, to the coven."

julie

"Coven?" the word tumbled out of my mouth with more shock attached to it than I had intended.

"Julie, you're a hearth witch at heart. Haven't you always been good with herbs and spices? Don't you understand how to make magic with ingredients? Emma Jane was the best hearth witch we've ever seen. We are, of course, good witches," Violet said then began pointing to the others. "Stitch witch," she said, pointing to Tootie, "soap witch," she said, pointing to Betty, "And I'm not so bad at healing. We practice good magic, and clearly, you belong with us."

I looked at the broom I was holding. The handle, much like the broom in Mrs. Aster's house, was engraved.

"It's too much for her to take in right now," Dr.

Franklin said. "She should just watch tonight then decide on her own. Let's not put any pressure on her."

"Agreed," another woman, Mrs. Bradley, said. She'd given me a brochure for makeup sales at the meeting. "Let her come to it in her own time, Tootie. We loved Emma Jane, but she isn't Emma Jane. We have to remember that...forget-me-not and all."

Tootie nodded. "Of course. Well, how about you have a seat and watch then, dear?" Tootie said, motioning for me to take a stump. "Do you mind?"

"N...no," I stammered, not sure if I should laugh, run off in fear, or hoist my broom and join them. I always ran pagan, but witchcraft? That was a new one even for me.

"Okay, girls," Tootie said, "let's have at it."

The women came to stand in a circle around the reflection pool.

"Sacred Grove, we witches of Chancellor gather under your limbs and offer you our love and protection," Betty called.

"Let no axe fall thee," Violet added.

"Let no machine shake thee," Dr. Franklin intoned.

"Let no man touch thee," Mrs. Bradley said.

"We sweep mankind's coveting eye away," Tootie added then nodded to the girls.

"Forever protected may you be," called the ladies as they began moving in a circle around the pool, sweeping the ground as they walked. "With love and magic, we protect these trees! With magic we entwine. With magic we enwind. With magic we bring here. Let no foulness enter here! So mote it be. Thank ye!"

And just like that, the women's auxiliary of Chancellor, who were, apparently a secret coven, finished casting what appeared to be a protection spell on the little grove.

I sat there in stunned silence.

A moment later, the ladies relaxed and began clasping one another, hugging, offering kisses, and chatting about their next get-together.

Several ladies stopped to say good-bye, leaving one by one, until Violet, Tootie, and Betty remained.

"You see, nothing to it," Tootie said.

"But who are you praying to? God? A witch goddess? The devil?"

At the last part, all three of them laughed. "The universe, my dear, is infinite in its love. We pray to love, to compassion, to gratitude. We evoke the mystery of love and magic, which is all. You should join us. You have the gift. Thank you again for the cupcakes. They worked splendidly," she said, and with a wave, left me standing in the grove, alone once more.

Not wanting to see what might show up next under those trees, I headed across the street toward my new home. I went inside, flipping on the lights, then locked the door behind me.

"Honey, I'm home," I called, jokingly, once more.

I was startled, however, when a stiff breeze blew in from the greenhouse, fluttering the cards in the recipe box which sat open on the counter. One of the cards jumped out and danced—as if a hand was pushing it—across the floor where it landed at my feet.

I bent to pick up the card.

Reading over the ingredients and the spell, I grinned. "Emma Jane, you're a genius," I called into the ether then headed into the kitchen.

horatio

"Stop fidgeting," Viola chided. "Everything looks great."

She was right. The lobby of the old theater had never looked more beautiful. Flower arrangements filled the place with the sweet scents of roses, carnations, and lilies. The brass on the bar glistened. The bartender served the well-dressed guests glass after glass of Blushing Grape wine. The aromas of butter and garlic filled the room. The chefs were preparing hors d'oeuvres for after the ceremony. A sweets display, which featured a cute little sign noting it was a "preview" of the reopening of Green Earth Apothecary and SerendipiTEA Gardens, was garnering a lot of attention. Town socialites and theater bugs munched on Julie's sweets while we all waited for the ceremony to begin.

"It's not that," I said, distracted. I checked my watch again. No Julie. No Dad. Where was everyone? Clearly, Julie had been by, but where was she? My need for her to be there, for her strong presence, for her support, weighed on me. How was it someone I was just getting to know suddenly meant so much to me, occupied so much of my headspace?

"She'll be back," Viola whispered.

Of course Viola would figure it out. I grinned at her.

The door opened. It was the mayor. Great, now we'd definitely have to get started. He paused, shaking hands and chatting with everyone as he worked his way toward the theater doors.

"Here, let me fix your tie," Viola said, turning me. Just like Mom might have done, Viola straightened my tie with a stiff jerk then adjusted the little grape leaf and purple rose corsage on my lapel.

"Easy," I said lightly, but I noticed then that my voice seemed to echo over the crowd. The room had become silent.

We turned to find Dad standing in the doorway.

I hadn't spoken to him since the night of The Grove meeting.

"Dad," Viola called cheerfully. Passing me a knowing *don't get into it with him now* look, Viola crossed the room and linked her arm in his.

Seeing that my dad wasn't there to make a scene, the others started talking again.

"Hey," someone said lightly, setting a soft hand on my shoulder.

I turned to find Julie standing there. She was wearing a stunning black dress, her hair pulled up into a loose bun at the back, her dreads wound loosely. She looked so beautiful.

"You look amazing," I gasped.

She laughed. "You too. How long before you get started?"

I was just about to answer her when the theater lights dimmed. "Um, now."

Julie nodded. "Okay, I'll catch you after then," she said then headed toward her sweets display. As I watched her go, I had to be mindful I was about to stand on stage in front of a hundred people. Admiring Julie's curvy body even a second more could prove embarrassing for me.

"Ready dear?" Professor Lane asked then, looping her arm in mine. "When was the last time you were on this stage?"

"*Peter Pan*."

"Oh, yes. You made a very convincing pirate."

"I didn't have any lines," I replied.

Professor Lane laughed. "Really?"

"I was Tinker Bell," Viola said from behind us. I looked back to see Viola gently guiding Dad into the theater. Maybe it was just my imagination, but he looked pale and thinner. The last few days, it seemed, had been hard on him. Viola said he hadn't come into the office nor had he been by the restaurant. He just stayed at home. No one had even seen him.

"And you were stunning," Professor Lane said, smiling at her. "We do need to get you back on the stage, my dear. Don't you think so, Aaron? Viola always took after her mother. She's a natural."

My dad muttered something incomprehensible in assent.

"Let's get you into place, shall we?" Professor Lane said. With that, she led me toward the stage. How many times had I sat beside my mother in those old theater seats as she directed work, watched a performance, or simply provided her expertise? Now I was there to honor her memory, and nothing made me feel sadder and more proud in the very same moment.

CHAPTER 19

I watched as the crowd entered the theater, the ushers shutting the doors behind them, then got to work.

A phone call to Viola had done the trick, and soon I had the green light to put my plan into action. Working quickly and quietly, I set up my display. First, I set out the cupcake stands and strung the display with blue lights and grape vines. I then worked quickly pulling out the massive box of cupcakes I'd made that morning. The cupcakes, made from Blushing Grape Vineyard's ice wine, Frozen Kisses, and sweetened with apricots, had turned out perfectly.

The bartender had already started setting out wine stands all around the room as the caterer prepared the rich feast of hors d'oeuvres that would follow the renaming ceremony. The chefs, who I soon discovered were students from the culinary school, worked at stations preparing bacon-wrapped scallops, duck foie gras, shrimp ceviche, stuffed squash blossoms, and a myriad of other culinary delights. With a little arm wrestling, my cupcakes were now the singular dessert at the event—and with reason. If I could get Aaron Hunter to taste one, everything in Horatio's world had a chance to go back to right.

My cupcakes, the white frosting sprinkled with crystal sugar and topped with a sugared grape, looked perfect. Emma Jane's recipe for the wine cupcakes, and its corresponding spell, would work. If only I could get all the Hunters to cooperate.

I turned to my display.

"Do your work," I whispered to the little cupcakes then repeated the spell that was on the recipe card once more:

Let all that's frozen come to pass
And sugar thaw that heart at last
Where broken hearts have torn away
And shattered love one autumn's day
Let butter enlighten and renew
And eggs rebirth a heart now true
The heart that's frozen passing grim
And be like love born again.

I was ready.

A half an hour later, the doors opened, and the crowd entered the lobby. I lifted the tray on which I'd set three perfect cupcakes and three glasses of Frozen Kisses ice wine. Moving carefully, I made my way through the crowd toward Viola, Horatio, and Aaron.

"Hi, Julie," Viola said sweetly, but I could see her eyes were red and puffy.

I was suddenly very sorry I'd missed Horatio's speech.

I turned and smiled at him. His eyes too were wet with tears. How special their mom must have been to them. As the thought struck me, I considered my feelings toward my own mother, buried under the hurricane of events that currently surrounded me. Bittersweet, more than anything, described the lingering feelings I felt toward her. I took a deep breath and refocused on the Hunters before I got pulled too deeply down the well of my own thoughts.

"They're serving Frozen Kisses," I said, handing a wine flute to each of them. Without looking up, Mr. Hunter took the glass from me.

"Mom's favorite," Viola said softly.

"And, I made something special," I added, pressing the silver platter forward. On the platter were the three perfect cupcakes. "I prepared these with the ice wine. I paired it with apricots. I think the marriage came out perfectly, but you're the experts. Mind trying and let me know how I did?"

Horatio was the first to take a taste. A small bit of frosting clung to the corner of his mouth. I had to restrain myself from wanting to lick it off. Instead, I dabbed it quickly with my fingertips. From the look in his eyes, I could see Horatio's mind had drifted to the same place mine had.

"Perfect," he said. "It really does taste like the wine. Try it, Vi."

"I just cut carbs this morning," she said, but her eyes sparkled as she eyed the cupcake.

"Just one bite?" I said nicely. "Just a taste to see if I've got it right?"

Looking like all she wanted was someone to give her a good reason, Viola tasted the confection, sighing deeply as she did so. "God, Julie. You're going to make everyone in Chancellor fat."

I laughed. "Well, these are the first official Green Earth Apothecary and SerendipiTEA brand cupcakes. I've named this one the Eleonora."

I was about to try to convince Mr. Hunter to take a bite when Viola turned to her dad and practically shoved the cupcake into his mouth.

"Try it," she said.

He smiled politely as he chewed.

"No hard feelings, Mr. Hunter. You're welcome to use my parking lot in the evening after I close the shop, by the way. So tell me, how did I do? Do you like the cupcake?"

Aaron Hunter stared at me with his steely blue eyes like he was considering whether or not I was trying to be an ass or if I was actually attempting to be nice. But then, I saw it. A kind of sparkle passed his gaze, a momentary iridescence glimmering over the eye and then it was gone. And a second later, his face softened. And his eyes...well, the color suddenly looked different. Warmer. Like the ice had, indeed, melted.

"It's delicious, Julie. My wife would have loved it," he said. He paused for a moment, sipped the wine, then said, "And thank you for the offer. I...I'm sorry for how I acted. I'm not myself these days," he added, then his face twisted. "Horatio," he said then, turning to his son. But he seemed at a loss for words.

Wordlessly, I took the wine flutes from their hands then stood and watched in delighted awe as father embraced his son.

"I'm sorry," I heard Aaron whisper. "I'm so proud of you. I'm sorry. I love you."

"I love you too," Horatio replied.

Now my eyes were watering. It had worked. I closed my eyes. *Thank you, Emma Jane.*

Before I knew what had happened, I felt arms wrap around me, and I was drowned in Horatio's heavenly cologne. I cast an eye at Viola and Aaron who were hugging, whispering softly to one another.

"You," Horatio whispered, but that was all he said. He had no way to know what I had done, not really, but that *you* was both caring and appreciative all in one breath. "Thank you for coming here tonight."

"There's nowhere I'd rather be," I replied softly.

After a moment, he let me go.

"I have to thank everyone for coming. Can I stop by tonight after the party?"

I nodded.

"Save me another one of those cupcakes," he said, winking to me, then went to work the room.

The whole lobby shimmered with golden light, and I could feel love and joy emanating from everyone. It seemed, at least for the moment, that there was nothing a magical cupcake couldn't set to right.

IT WAS CLOSE TO MIDNIGHT WHEN THE Mercedes SUV pulled up outside. Soft music pulsed out from the speakers attached to my phone, and I had everything ready...candles, champagne, strawberries, and two more of the magical cupcakes.

I opened the door before he even knocked.

"Hi," I said softly, closing the door behind him.

"Wow, look at this place," Horatio breathed. The whole shop was bathed in candlelight, the warm glow making the place feel magical. "Julie," he began, turning to me, but before he could say another word, I wrapped my arms around his neck and pressed my lips against his. They were soft, warm, and held the lingering tastes of wine and sugar. I kissed him hard, my tongue roving inside his mouth, wanting to absorb his sweetness. We kissed for what felt like forever. Finally seeing stars, I pulled away and giggled, steadying myself.

"I have spots in front of my eyes. I don't know if it is the wine, the cupcakes, or just...you. But something about this night has just seemed..."

"Magical?" I offered.

"That's the perfect word."

"How about I bewitch you just a little more," I replied as I gazed into his eyes.

Pulling me close, Horatio kissed my neck. "You smell like vanilla," he whispered, "and taste sweet," he said, kissing me. "And salty," he added after another kiss, "and..."

"And?"

"And I can't get enough," he whispered in my ear.

"Then you're not trying hard enough," I said.

With that, Horatio gently lifted me. I wrapped my legs around his waist. Without another word, he carried me to the back where we fell into one another, at the very witching hour of night, in the sweetest of rapture.

epilogue

"Thanks so much! enjoy them," I called as a mother guided her daughter out the front door. The little girl was carrying a crinkly brown paper wrapper full of the freshly toasted sugared walnuts I had warming in a repurposed antique popcorn machine. It was the week of my grand opening, and the Chancellor Christmas bazaar, and the shop was packed. I'd completely outdone myself decorating for Christmas. I'd managed to fit seven fully-decorated Christmas trees in the small shop, and the greenhouse was loaded with amazing pink, peppermint-striped, and ruby-red poinsettias. Violet's granddaughter, Lacey, a student at the college, had started working with me the week before, and was doing a fantastic job. I watched in quiet satisfaction as she raced back and forth from the kitchen to the tea garden in the greenhouse serving eggnog, frosted sugar cookies, peppermint or cranberry tea, and gallons of hot chocolate. The tea house was a hit.

"Julie," my dad said. "I think this dip might be bad. It tastes weird," he added as he looked from his pretzel to the jar in his hand.

"That's because it's lemon peel face cream," I replied with a laugh.

"Face cream?" my dad said, looking puzzled.

"Don't worry. It's organic," I replied.

My dad laughed out loud and set the jar down.

Just then the bell above the door rang, and Alice, Rayne, and Horatio entered. Everyone was bundled up and covered in a light dusting of snow.

"Ready?" Alice asked.

"Jules, it's so busy here. You sure you have time?" Horatio asked, casting a glance around the store.

"Go," Lacey called as she passed through with a tray. "We can spare you an hour."

"Horatio! Nice to see you again," Dad called.

"Nice to see you too, Mister Dayton. Mind if I borrow Julie for a bit?"

"Take an hour, Julie. We've got you covered. Oh! And I have something for you. I almost forgot." Going behind the counter, he pulled out a bag and handed it to me.

"What is it?" I asked.

"Ice skates. They belonged to your mother. You're the same shoe size, right? Don't you remember when she used to take you down to Lily Hill Park? You went every winter when you were a kid...well, until Mom's back started to give her problems. You know she wanted to be a professional ice skater? She was part of the Chasing Stars skate team. I just found her trophies and photos the other day when I was packing some things up."

Chasing stars. I slowly unwrapped the package and looked at the ice skates. They were white and decorated with faded silver stars. All at once, memories of my mother and me ice skating flooded over me like they'd been unlocked from somewhere deep within my memory. All these years I thought she'd wanted me to play it safe because that's what she did. I'd either forgotten or never knew that she, too, had wanted more. And in that moment, I understood my mother in a way I never had before.

"Do you remember how to skate?" Horatio asked.

I shook my head. "No, but I'll try," I said then started pulling on my coat. Following behind Rayne and Alice, Horatio and I headed outside.

Main Street was closed to traffic and had been transformed into a winter wonderland. The snow and ice sculpture competitions were well underway. Fat snowflakes drifted downward. A sleigh pulled excited revelers past, the jingle bells ringing merrily. Across the street, Milt Row and the other husbands of the coven witches were standing around a bonfire as they sold Christmas trees from a lot just near The Grove.

"Where's Viola?" I asked.

"Stuck," Horatio answered. "Falling Waters is booked."

"We'll get her out today yet, if I have something to say about it," Rayne said, gazing longingly toward the restaurant, his eyes twinkling. I looked from Horatio to Alice. Neither of them seemed to notice the expression on Rayne's face.

"You going to spend the whole day on your butt again?" Alice asked Horatio jokingly.

"Hey, I spent the week practicing so I wouldn't look like a total failure in front of Julie. Thanks for completely shattering the image."

Alice laughed. "Sorry!"

Rayne sighed heavily then turned his gaze from the restaurant.

Walking arm in arm with Horatio, my mind got busy.

"And just why are you grinning like that?" Horatio asked, leaning in to kiss my cheek. "My sweet," he added, nibbling my ear.

"Oh. No reason," I said, but I was already thinking through the recipes in the box. My heart was brimming with love. I wanted everyone to feel just like I did. Maybe Rayne and Viola just needed a push in the right direction.

Well, that was nothing a magical cupcake couldn't solve.

CONTINUE *THE CHANCELLOR FAIRY TALES* WITH *THE FAIRY GODFATHER.*

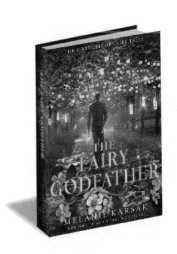

Available on Amazon

about the author

New York Times and *USA Today* bestselling author Melanie Karsak is the author of *The Celtic Blood Series, The Road to Valhalla Series, The Celtic Rebels Series, Steampunk Red Riding Hood, Steampunk Fairy Tales* and many more works of fiction. The author currently lives in Florida with her husband and two children.

    amazon.com/author/melaniekarsak

    facebook.com/authormelaniekarsak

    instagram.com/karsakmelanie

    pinterest.com/melaniekarsak

    youtube.com/@authormelaniekarsak

    bookbub.com/authors/melanie-karsak

also by melanie karsak

THE CELTIC BLOOD SERIES:

Highland Raven

Highland Blood

Highland Vengeance

Highland Queen

THE CELTIC REBELS SERIES:

Queen of Oak: A Novel of Boudica

Queen of Stone: A Novel of Boudica

Queen of Ash and Iron: A Novel of Boudica

THE ROAD TO VALHALLA SERIES:

Shield-Maiden: Under the Howling Moon

Shield-Maiden: Under the Hunter's Moon

Shield-Maiden: Under the Thunder Moon

Shield-Maiden: Under the Blood Moon

Shield-Maiden: Under the Dark Moon

THE SHADOWS OF VALHALLA SERIES:

Shield-Maiden: Winternights Gambit

Shield-Maiden: Gambit of Blood

Shield-Maiden: Gambit of Shadows

Shield-Maiden: Gambit of Swords

THE HARVESTING SERIES:

The Harvesting

Midway

The Shadow Aspect

Witch Wood

The Torn World

STEAMPUNK FAIRY TALES:

Curiouser and Curiouser: Steampunk Alice in Wonderland

Ice and Embers: Steampunk Snow Queen

Beauty and Beastly: Steampunk Beauty and the Beast

Golden Braids and Dragon Blades: Steampunk Rapunzel

THE RED CAPE SOCIETY

Wolves and Daggers

Alphas and Airships

Peppermint and Pentacles

Bitches and Brawlers

Howls and Hallows

Lycans and Legends

THE AIRSHIP RACING CHRONICLES:

Chasing the Star Garden

Chasing the Green Fairy

Chasing Christmas Past

THE CHANCELLOR FAIRY TALES:

The Glass Mermaid

The Cupcake Witch

The Fairy Godfather

The Vintage Medium

The Book Witch

Find these books and more on Amazon!

Made in the USA
Middletown, DE
21 December 2023

46397458R00087